For my

A fictionalized version of times past,
but some of it will be familiar to you.

TO ROSEWOOD

Love.
A. Peg

Pegeen Brennan

Pegeen Brennan

Kilpoola Books

Note for Librarians: a cataloguing record for this book that includes Dewey Decimal Classification and US Library of Congress numbers is available from the Library and Archives of Canada. The complete cataloguing record can be obtained from their online database at: www.collectionscanada.ca/amicus/index-e.html
ISBN 1-4120-4752-8
Printed in Victoria, BC, Canada

Layout and design of cover by Meltem Cankaya
Author's photo by Sandy Gabriel

TRAFFORD

Offices in Canada, USA, Ireland, UK and Spain
This book was published *on-demand* in cooperation with Trafford Publishing.
On-demand publishing is a unique process and service of making a book available for retail sale to the public taking advantage of on-demand manufacturing and Internet marketing. On-demand publishing includes promotions, retail sales, manufacturing, order fulfilment, accounting and collecting royalties on behalf of the author.
Book sales for North America and international:
Trafford Publishing, 6E–2333 Government St.,
Victoria, BC v8t 4p4 CANADA
phone 250 383 6864 (toll-free 1 888 232 4444)
fax 250 383 6804; email to orders@trafford.com
Book sales in Europe:
Trafford Publishing (uk) Ltd., Enterprise House, Wistaston Road Business Centre,
Wistaston Road, Crewe, Cheshire cw2 7rp UNITED KINGDOM
phone 01270 251 396 (local rate 0845 230 9601)
facsimile 01270 254 983; orders.uk@trafford.com
Order online at:
www.trafford.com/robots/04-2560.html

10 9 8 7 6 5 4 3

TO ROSEWOOD

For my sister Sandy,
who dared to be a Daniel

And in memory of our aunt and uncle,
Dorothy and Sam Brennan

TO ROSEWOOD

ONE

MY MOTHER DIED OF POLIO WHEN I WAS SEVEN. ACTUALLY, I WAS thirty-eight days away from turning eight. I came home from school one afternoon to find our part of my uncle's house empty. She called me from upstairs. I had never before seen her in bed during the day. My little sister lay quietly beside her. My mother asked me to take her out so she could sleep a little. She had never spoken to me in such a subdued voice.

As she spoke, the baby scrambled up and raised her arms to me. I lifted her up and took her downstairs. She was fourteen months old. She could walk really well. She gripped my middle finger and I went slow. She raised each foot in an exaggerated step at every weed and rock in the barnyard. I don't remember where my other sisters were—one older, one between me and the baby. We should all have walked home from school together. But that day there was only me.

Back in the house, I followed my mother's instructions. I poured orange juice from a jar. I left the baby in the kitchen with the door closed. One hand behind my mother's head to raise it from the pillow. The other to hold the glass to her lips. Her head was heavy; it was hard to get the glass close enough. And that was all.

Next morning our father came to the room where we were sleeping. My sisters were with me then. The oldest had the baby next to her. He sat on the bed where I lay with my younger sister. His head bowed over all of us. His elbows on his knees. His fingers moved back and forth against each other in the semi-darkness. "Your mother is dead."

My oldest sister hoisted the baby aside and sat up. "Has she gone to Heaven?"

I think my father said, "Yes."

Infantile paralysis. It wasn't supposed to affect adults. My mother had taken us all to the Hallowe'en party at the school a few days before. That's where she picked it up, everyone said, but how come she got it and not any of the children? Not even the baby?

The sign on the big wooden gate said, "POLIOMYELITIS." People from the neighbouring farms came by to read it. They brought paper and pencil to write it down because it was a word no one had ever heard before. And later they came with wheelbarrows which they had to leave at the gate. My uncle brought them in, and they were full of food. Because of the quarantine we were not allowed to go out, not even to the store up the road. The only part of the food I can remember is the butter tarts.

Because of the poliomyelitis my mother had to be buried right away. The next day. I went up the stairs by myself in the evening. I wanted to see her, to make sure she was really dead. The door was closed, locked. I put my eye to the keyhole. I could see the bed with her shape on it, with bedclothes pulled over her head. The glass on the stand beside the bed still had a little orange juice in it.

Despite the quarantine, some aunts and uncles came. The aunts hugged our father and cried. He was their youngest brother, just thirty. Our mother was almost a year younger. Her coffin was in the yard, closed. It was on a slant because the ground wasn't level where they had put it.

I sat with my three sisters on the bare cement that ran the length of the house. The oldest one held the baby on her lap. We leaned into each other. No one said anything to us.

The minister was there, from his church the other side of the general store. He was out beside the coffin on a small hump of ground. When he finished talking, he came over to us and stood looking down. He seemed ready to say something but nothing came out. He stood over us, shaking his head slowly. Then he reached into his pocket and brought out something which he gave to my oldest sister. We all saw it. It was a dime.

The coffin was taken away immediately in a black hearse. The few cars followed it out the gate and we were left alone. Our oldest sister let us look a long time at the ten-cent piece before she put it in the pocket of her coat.

Some time later there was a headstone engraved with: "Kathleen Anne—Beloved Wife of Terrence Cassidy." The four of us were separated and handed over to various aunts and uncles. Our father went west to work in the coal

9

mines. A story was told by the aunt and uncle who got the baby. When she was about four years old, they took her to the graveyard. She ran right over to our mother's grave, put her arms around the tombstone and said, "I like this white one."

Our oldest sister didn't get along with any of the aunts and uncles who took her. Before long, someone managed to send her out to our father. We heard from her a few times. They were in a little mining town, the highest town in all of Canada. And our father had two horses.

I, and my sister next youngest, lived with several of the aunts and uncles, going back and forth from one family to the other. Sometimes we lived in the country; sometimes we lived in the town. Finally, the nicest of all the uncles, the one just older than our father, got married and we went to live with him and his new wife at our grandparents' place, Rosewood Farm. He had had to quit medical school because he didn't have enough money to continue. He had things in pickle jars in a room upstairs, things like fungus plants, and snakes, and the tiny body of a lamb before it was born. There was even a person's heart, floating in a reddish-brown liquid. The new aunt always called that room "the museum." My uncle had gone back to Rosewood Farm because our grandfather was old and needed help to run it.

We all lived in the big white farmhouse, but not exactly together. My sister was downstairs with our grandparents, I was upstairs with our uncle and aunt. We went there the middle of May. That was the year I was ten. It was my seventh change of school.

By then our uncle had decided to do market gardening

because there was so little income from the farm. He had planted many of the usual crops—hay, grain, corn, potatoes, turnips. He also grew whatever vegetables and berries he could sell on a route that took him to the major resorts and stores along the lakes and to all the summer cottages on the way. Our grandmother kept my sister in the house to do inside chores, but I was expected to help with everything at the barn—milking, feeding, moving manure—as well as work with the vegetables and berries. But my help was not enough. That is how I came to know Old Ed.

Old Ed lived about three quarters of a mile down the road, not far from the highway. He walked up every morning, his little black dog following at his heels. His left arm hung at his side. The hand was white and flat, the fingers stretched down, unmoving. He smiled as he came to where I was waiting to start the hoeing. As he took up the hoe my uncle had sharpened for him he always said something about a farm he used to work at where you couldn't find a single stone if you needed one to pound an axle into place or knock a bull snake on the head, not like here with the rocks dulling a hoe before even an hour's work. I watched as he seized the hoe with his good hand, maneuvered the handle into the crook of his arm in just the way I remembered my mother holding the broom when she brushed the sweepings into the dust pan. He could hoe fast that way too. And he never seemed to cut off any cabbage plants or strawberry runners, or sprouts of squash or beans the way I sometimes did. Another thing that really impressed me about Old Ed was what he did when he started to work: as he crooked the handle of the hoe into place, he would turn to his dog and say, "Well, Bonnie, I

11

guess you'd better be trotting along home now." She would get up from where she was sitting, shake herself free of dust, and start off. I watched her go down the lane and head out onto the road, her nose low to the ground as though she was tracking the way they had come. He'd laugh and say, "That's a good little dog." He whistled all the time he hoed. Up one row, down the other, always whistling.

The other aunts and uncles came to visit sometimes. Mostly on Sundays. After dinner we would hear them talking—the men out around the barn, the women as they rested after dishes. They didn't seem to notice we were there. "It's just as well she died, you know." "Yes, if she'd lived she would've been crippled." "What kind of a life would that've been for him and the girls?" "They're better off this way." "Yes, when it was that bad... Imagine growing up with a paralyzed mother."

Then I thought of Old Ed and walked away trying to whistle the way he did. But it didn't really sound like him. It was more like just a whisper of a whistle.

TWO

THE SUMMER I WAS EIGHT MY HEADACHES BEGAN. I REMEMBER MY sister asking our father, "Has Mommy gone to Heaven?" and I knew she had not, because I could hear her voice inside me. She told me to say thank you for everything anyone did for me or gave to me. I was to learn to write well so I could send letters if I got any presents. She wanted me to do as I was told, even if it were my older sister who was telling me. And she said it was a good idea to be helpful to everyone so they would like me. If they liked me it would be better for me. And I was to be clean and keep things neat. Everyone else maybe thought she was in Heaven, but I knew where she really was.

When we were staying with Aunt Jane in Barrie, the next town to the south of Orillia, the town which was closest to Rosewood, I tried hard to be nice to everyone. This aunt, our father's oldest sister, was plump and pleasant and we felt good when we were with her. But she had two children of her own. Angie (her real name was Angelica) was sixteen; Mint (his real name was Clement) was thirteen. The house was very small. The flat roof along the front looked as though it was pushing the walls down into the grass. Our aunt and uncle used one bedroom; Angie and my sister and I slept all together in the other. Mint had to have a cot made up for him every night in a corner of the main room, which was already crowded with the dining table and chairs, a small sofa, and a china cabinet.

One night, after we had been there about a week, Angie made me lie in the middle, next to her. She spread her legs and pulled me close, and rubbed against me. I felt that this was not a nice thing to do. I didn't like her sallow freckled face and the way spit oozed out of the corner of her mouth and I didn't like her rough hairs to be touching me down there. But I could hear my mother's voice: "Be nice to her."

The next day she didn't look at me or let on that anything had happened. When she saw me standing in front of the dresser trying to put a barrette in my hair for school, she said, "Why are you looking in the mirror? You're such an ugly thing." I didn't say anything, and I didn't tell anyone about the place in my head that hurt.

Aunt Jane and Uncle Elliot went out nearly every night to mission. That was what they called the service at the Pentecostal Church. It wasn't really a church. It was a small hall, with a stage at the front, and rows of chairs. On Saturdays and Sundays they took us with them. It was strange for us because we had never gone to a church before. The pastor talked loud and he walked fast back and forth across the platform. His arms never stopped moving. The

14

people talked too. They said things like "Praise the Lord!" "Hallelujah!" "Amen!" and "Glory be to God!" Aunt Jane didn't say any of those things. She just kept saying, "Jesus, Jesus," real low. And Uncle Elliot didn't say anything at all. He sat still with his eyes closed. Maybe praying. Or maybe because his eyes were sore. He had told us there wasn't enough light for the close work he did at the tannery. Some of the people stood up and made short speeches about being saved by Jesus and about how they used to be sinners but now were cleansed in the blood. It was all sort of lively and the singing was good too. My favourite hymns were "What a Friend we Have in Jesus," because it felt so friendly, and "Dare to be a Daniel," because it was so fast and definite. But the two pieces were telling me different things. The first one said that Jesus would do everything for a person— "all our sins and griefs to bear,"—while the second one said to be like Daniel—"Dare to stand alone. Dare to have a purpose firm, and Dare to make it known."

As I sat in my chair just below the stage, where all the children were crowded together, I leaned into the pain in the middle of my forehead. And I thought of the night-times with Angie and I wondered if that was what sin was and I wondered what Friend Jesus would think, but then I remembered my mother's words, and it seemed all right, more like being a Daniel.

That is just one part about Angie. There's a lot more about her. She made us go downtown to the fruit store to take messages to the Italian man who worked there. Mostly it was to tell him when she'd be home alone. She told us about going to the gravel pit with him and he didn't even wait for her to get her underpants off. She called them

15

step-ins. They were what grownups wore; we still had to wear bloomers. Anyway, he couldn't wait and he went right through the opening of the leg. And she told about another man who came when Aunt Jane and Uncle Elliot were at mission. When she wouldn't let him do it, he threw all his French safes in the stove. She had a way of rolling her eyes and letting her mouth sag. She said it was hard for her when she started having her monthlies because then she had to be careful. She also said she could hear the creaking of bedsprings in the next room at night and it wasn't fair. She had a right to have fun too.

Mint was a lot nicer. He was like a big brother who looked after us and he spent lots of time wheeling me around on the crossbar of his bike. He had one crippled up foot, kind of humped in the middle. It gave him a real limp but you couldn't notice it at all when he was on his bike. It was bumpy on the metal bar but it was a good feeling too. With my hands tight on the handlebars inside his, I could lean sideways against his chest. That way, he had one arm behind me and one in front. It was like being in a safe cage. He took us for rides in his wagon too, down a big hill at the end of the block, by the Orange Crush factory. And in the winter he got us to help him sell Christmas trees. He had a big bob sled for that.

One night when Aunt Jane and Uncle Elliot were at mission we were home alone with him. Angie was supposed to be looking after us but she had gone off somewhere. The bathroom was in the basement and I was down there going to the toilet, but the lights went off. I tried to find the stairs in the dark but Mint grabbed me just before I got there. I almost got away by holding onto the rail and pushing at him. I thought that because of his crumpled foot I could get free and run up the stairs. But he held on tight and half carried, half hoisted me up. He hauled me across the kitchen, flung me on the bed in our room and jerked at my bloomers. He held me down with one hand and pulled at them with the other. My throat seemed to swell and get stiff. I don't know whether I made a noise or not. I couldn't move except to bang at him with my fists.

Then he was gone. I felt him slide off me. I heard him grunting, and a scrabbling noise, too. The door banged shut. I heard the key turn in the lock. "You stay out!" Then my sister was at the bed. "I got him by the hair from behind. I had to jump up on him." She crawled up beside me, breathing fast. "I locked him out." I pulled up my bloomers and straightened my skirt.

He made noises in the other room. Then he pounded on the door. My sister yelled, "You stay out!"

"We're going to send you out west to your dad, you know. Ma's already sent him a letter."

He rattled the doorknob. "And if he won't take you, you can't stay here. You'll have to go to the orphanage!"

We didn't say anything. We just sat together on the bed in the dark.

We heard Angie come in. She said something to Mint and he muttered something back but it was too low for us to hear. She didn't even try the bedroom door.

Then Aunt Jane and Uncle Elliot were home. We could hear their voices better. "It was a wonderful meeting," she said.

"Yes," he said. "Four new people in the congregation gave themselves to our Saviour tonight. You two should have been there to see it."

17

We could hear our aunt walking past our door toward the kitchen. "The little girls would have liked it too. We sang 'Dare to be a Daniel.'"

THREE

NONE OF US WENT BY OUR REAL NAMES. WE ALL HAD NICKNAMES
and we did our best to hang onto them. Our oldest sister
was Ruthanne but it was shortened to Annie. I was Bubba.
I guess it came from Annie trying to say "baby" when I was
born. My real name was Virginnia and I hated it because I
thought they had named me after tobacco. On top of that,
my dad had been the one to register me and he spelled it
wrong. With two n's. My younger sister was Puggy because
of her short, turned-up nose. Her real name was Sylvia.
And the baby was Poppy. I'm not sure why. Her real name
was Aline.

Of course, everyone used our proper names at school, but
the two of us hung onto Bubba and Puggy as secret names
for each other, even after we went to stay at Rosewood. Our
nicest uncle still called us Bubba and Puggy. That shows
how nice he was. Maybe he understood because of his own
nickname. His real name was Walter, but because that was

his only name, he took "T" as a middle initial when he started highschool so he could pretend he had a second name. Just to make fun of him, the family started calling him "Tee." So to us he was always Uncle Tee. He said he never liked Walter anyway.

When we went back to live at Rosewood Farm, we found out that the boy on the farm across the road also had a nickname or, rather, two. They were what he called himself. An old man had lived there as a bachelor for years. Puggy and I had to go through his place when we took the shortcut to school; the long way around—south to the townline, east to the highway, then north to the school— was three miles. The route through Old Man Carson's place, then across several bush lots, fields, and pastures, was half the distance. We would hurry through his yard, afraid we might see him, half hoping we might. The house was an old, unpainted, ramshackle place, its verandah piled with junk. Old tubs and pails, broken tools, rusty pieces of metal. A sign over his door read "Full Course Meals Fifty Cents." Uncle Tee said it was something he'd had for a long time because you hadn't been able to get a meal for fifty cents for years. The yard too was full of junk. Parts of implements mostly, such as mowers and scufflers, broken and rusted. We felt relieved when we slipped past the sugar shack and into the safety of the tall trees of his maple bush.

Some time that spring the old man got married. His wife was Mrs. Tapping, now Mrs. Carson, who had a son about our age. The old man told Uncle Tee himself. When we first heard the news we thought it would be fun having him to walk to school with, then maybe we would

20

find out something about the old man. But the son didn't go to school. At first we saw him only occasionally, if he happened to be outside when we cut through the yard. He had a droopy mouth and bugged-out eyes. He was short and plump and couldn't seem to make his arms and legs move right.

One day he was standing by the sugar shack when we came home from school. We were a little late because we had stopped to pick wild strawberries in the pasture on the other side of the maple bush. We had quite a few in our lunch boxes. We walked a little faster as we came by him but he stepped out onto the trail. We both said "Hello" and moved around him, one on each side. He laughed a long silly kind of laugh with his head tilted up in a funny way. At the same time he leapt ahead of us and slapped his hands against the outside of his legs. Then he stopped and looked at us, first at Puggy, then at me. "Hello" we both said again.

"Helly, Helly," he shouted and leapt on ahead. Then he spun around, veering off to one side, and stood still in front of us.

"What's your name?" Puggy said. She had come alongside me and stood close.

He raised his fingers to the side of his mouth, punched his cheek a couple of times, and said, "Siddy, Siddy Tappy." He ran off then, stumbling and laughing ahead of us, yelling, "Siddy Tappy. Siddy Tappy."

We followed him across the yard. Puggy said maybe we should give him some of our strawberries. Then the door to the verandah opened and a skinny lady stepped out. She wore a long, brown dress and had wispy, brown hair. She called: "Sydney, you come in the house now. Don't bother those girls." She went back in and shut the door.

He didn't stop running. He moved across the yard in his stumbly way. As he slowed at the steps he turned to look at us. "Whash ya mame? Siddy Tappy. Siddy Tappy."

We saw him often after that. He would be somewhere in the laneway in the mornings, somewhere around the sugar shack when we came by in the afternoons. His greeting was always, "Whash ya mame? Siddy Tappy." Sometimes when he said, "Whash ya mame?" we would cut in fast and tell him our names. I'd say, "I'm Bubba, and this is Puggy." But he paid no attention. He would just laugh and slap at his sides and say, "Siddy Tappy."

When school was finished in June he started coming over to our place, maybe when we were doing the milking in the morning, or when we were getting in the sheep in the evening. He would stand, mouth hanging open, watching whatever we were doing, then he would laugh, slap himself somewhere, run off to one side, and ease back again. Puggy and I thought he was like some kind of wild animal that was starting to get tame.

Uncle Tee told us the story about Old Man Carson and Siddy at one of the carnivals that came to town. It had rides and a midway and everything and there was a woman who set herself up as a reader of heads. She had on a blindfold and she would feel a person's head and then say what that person was like. Old Man Carson thought he would trick her by giving her Sydney to work on. He set him down on the stool and the lady started moving her fingers over his head. In a minute or two she stopped. Still with the blindfold on, she turned to the old man and said, "This child is a complete idiot." He didn't tell Uncle Tee himself. Mrs. Cook, who lived down past Old Ed's place near the highway, was there with her two boys and heard her say it.

Well, we already knew he wasn't very smart. There were a lot of things to show that, like the time the old man told him to bring in some water from a tub on the verandah. He'd have to break the ice first. He did break the ice but he used an axe to do it and he drove the blade right through the bottom of the tub. He managed to scoop out half a bucket before all the water ran out.

As Sydney got tamer, he would let us touch him. At first we just poked him a little to make him laugh, or we pretended to hold onto him to see what he would do. Sometimes he would run off, but usually just in a wobbly circle, and then he'd be back again. The first time he did that, he threw both arms in the air and sang out, "Oh Happy Day!" Puggy and I looked at each other. We were amazed. It was the beginning of a hymn we had learned at mission. "Oh, happy day, Oh happy day! Since Jesus washed my sins away."

It was some time near the end of summer before he got tame enough for us to tie him up. We got a long piece of rope out of the horse stable. We let him hold it first, and we played around with it so he'd get used to it. We told him it wasn't going to hurt. It was just for fun. We were in the passageway with the cows' stanchions on one side and the horses' mangers on the other. Puggy held him and poked him to make him laugh while I wound the rope around him and one of the stanchion posts. I tied it tight with a reef knot, the kind Uncle Tee had shown me how to make. It was easy to undo fast if you needed to. Then we ran off.

23

We actually went right outside the barn, by the chicken house.

"We'd better let him go," Puggy said. "He might be scared."

"He's not scared," I said. "He likes it. Let's wait a little longer."

And he did seem to like it. When we went back to let him loose, he went quiet until the rope was off, then he laughed and jumped up and down. He even took the rope from me and tried to wind it around himself. So we did it again, lots of times.

One day, while he was tied up, Aunt Helena called to us to come to the house because there was a letter from Annie. We went in to read it. We took it to our room, the one we shared upstairs. It was about some trouble she was having with our father. She said she wanted to leave because he was "treating her like a wife." She was going to write our Aunt Mary, our mother's sister in Oregon, to get help. We read it several times and we still couldn't understand. Puggy said, "Maybe he's making her cook and clean the house. She'd hate that."

Then Uncle Tee was calling us. "What is that boy doing in the barn? He's out there bawling his head off."

I shoved the letter into my pillowcase and ran out. From the doorstep we could hear him. Great long blubbering sounds.

He had worked himself loose enough to lie down on the cement. He was covered with chaff. He stopped crying when he saw us. We grabbed the rope right away but the knot was tight because he had pulled it so hard. When he was free, he stood up, slapped his thighs with one hand then the other. "You Bubba, you Pugga. You bad on Siddy. Siddy Tappy got mudda. You got no mudda."

Then he laughed. "You got no mudda." He ran out of the barn, across the barnyard, and down the lane, his arms flailing over his head. We could hear him all the way to their laneway. He was singing "Oh Happy Day," over and over.

FOUR

I USED TO THINK MY GRANDMOTHER WAS JESUS BECAUSE THE plaque that hung over the sink where my grandfather peeled potatoes said "Christ is the head of this house."

When we first arrived at Rosewood Farm only our grandfather was waiting for us. Uncle Tee had met us at the station in Orillia. It felt good to be on the ground again after three days and three nights on the train. Then we were in the back of a red truck. There were black canvas curtains that rolled down, with snap flaps at the very back, so it was like a little room with just one window we could look through and see our father and mother in the front with Uncle Tee. Grandad lifted us down, one after the other. He was excited and loud, but he got all our names straight right away. He was tall and thin. He had grey hair with a bare spot on top. His mouth was caved in as though his nose could reach his chin if he closed it hard. We had never seen anyone with no teeth before.

He shook hands with our mother and father and then hurried us three girls across the flat wide stone doorstep and into the kitchen. "Come and meet your grandmother," he said. So far, Grandma and Grandad had been words for faraway people, made a little more real once in a while by a letter or a parcel. Once there were wool scarves for the three of us. Mine was blue, Annie's and Puggy's were pink. One thing about being in the middle, I usually got the different colour. That was just to make the sizes easier to tell which was which. Not that it mattered with scarves. Our mother told us Grandma had knit them for us.

It was a hot day in August but the kitchen was even hotter because there was a fire on. A woman sat in a tall-backed rocking chair beside the stove. Our grandfather said, "Here she is. Say hello to your Grandma." She was a tiny person, wrapped in a yellow shawl, and she seemed even smaller because of the big chair. Annie and I said, "Hello Grandma." Puggy stayed behind me. The old lady smiled and her eyes crinkled, but she didn't say anything, just pulled the shawl tight around her shoulders. She looked as though she needed more heat than she was getting.

Then Uncle Tee came in with our parents and made introductions. "This is Lizzie. Lizzie Reynolds. She's looking in on Dad while Ma's away. Lizzie, this is my brother and his wife. And I guess you've met their girls already."

I looked back to my grandfather. He winked at me. So it was just a joke. Puggy took mother's hand and said, "Where's our real Grandma?" Uncle Tee explained that she was visiting Aunt Jane in a town called Barrie and that she'd be coming up by bus later and he'd go back into town

27

to get her. Maybe Aunt Jane and our cousin Angie would come too. It was Angie's birthday today; she was fourteen. That was why Grandma had gone down there.

The joke was a lot plainer when she did arrive. Annie and I watched out the kitchen window as the truck pulled up to the stone step. Uncle Tee came around to the right side and opened the door. Then he helped her out of the cab. We saw her head first, her grey hair pulled up in a bun on top. Her body bulged so big in her dress that I thought the flowers would burst right out of the material. There was nothing to say except that she was a big fat woman—at least three, maybe four, times the size of little Lizzie. Later we found out from a boy cousin that she weighed two hundred pounds. There was no one else with her. She had come back alone. She didn't look at all like Grandad except that she didn't have any teeth either.

I looked up at my grandfather as he crossed the kitchen to the door. "There she is," he said, and he winked at me again. I don't know if I did it right (it was hard not to let both eyes go shut) but I winked back. Then we all went out to meet her.

After she put her purse and a few parcels away in another room, she sat down at the kitchen table and started knitting on what looked like a big sock. The wool was red and black, twined together. Her hands made the needles move very fast. She could knit without looking at them at all. She kept knitting while our grandfather and Lizzie finished the cooking. Our mother set the table in the dining room and helped carry in the food. Grandad told Annie and me to count the people and then count the chairs to make sure there was the right number. There were only eight, so we had to bring in one from the kitchen.

There was no doubt, right from the start, that Grandma was the head of the house. As soon as the meal was over, with the last of the stewed prunes and tea biscuits, she pushed back from the table and said, "Dad, bring the Bible."

Grandad said, "Well, I don't think I know where it is."

She gave him a fierce look. "You must know where you put it the last time you read from it."

"No," he said. "I think you were the last one to use it." I thought I saw another wink but, if so, it wasn't at me but at Uncle Tee. They both had the beginnings of a smile.

"You mean you two haven't had prayer all the time I was away?" The fierce look was still on her face. "Well, go get it then. It'll be in by my bed."

That day was the first time I had ever heard of prayer. Or of the Bible, or of Jesus and God. I guess our mother and father knew about such things, but my sisters and I didn't. All we knew was Santa Claus, and we had actually met him. He made me sit on his knee when he came to our school concert. I had not quite turned six. I liked him right away because he had a present for me that I could tell by the shape was a gun. A gun was what I really needed because when Annie and Puggy and I rode around on long sticks chasing rustlers, we didn't have anything to shoot them with. But when I took off the wrapping, it wasn't a gun at all. It was a toy broom and dustpan set. I didn't think much of Santa Claus after that, but at least I knew he was real.

My grandmother must have thought Jesus and God were real too, and some other person called Lord, because she made all of us get down on our knees right beside our

29

chairs while she talked to them. That was what praying was. And that was after she read some pages from the Bible. And Grandad had to say a prayer too, after she was finished. They were both asking for things like faith and good health and happiness and they were both thankful that we had all come safely from the West to live with them. At the end of Grandad's prayer, he added something that started with "Our Father, who art in Heaven." It seemed to be something everyone knew (except me and my sisters) because they all joined in, even our father and mother. It ended with "Amen." I asked them afterwards how they knew it and they said they learned it when they were children.

Anyway, that is what happened after every meal. Often Grandma would try to get my mother and father to say a prayer too. But they always said no. She didn't ask Uncle Tee at all, probably because he had said no a long time ago.

There were other strange things that seemed to be connected to my grandmother and her Bible and her prayers. For one thing, she wouldn't let anyone smoke. She said it was sinful. So nobody did smoke around her, not that it affected our family because our mother had never smoked and our father used snuff. Except Uncle Tee. He always lit a cigarette as soon as he got in to drive the truck. Whenever she rode with him, she opened her window wide and kept brushing at her nose with her hand.

And no one was to do any work on Sunday. It was the day of the Lord, she said, and we were to keep it holy. She allowed the work that had to be done, such as milking, and feeding the stock, and cooking and dishes. Apart from those necessary jobs, everyone was supposed to read the Bible and pray. And it was just the Bible. Stories and newspapers were not allowed because they were for pleasure, and there wasn't supposed to be any pleasure on Sundays.

She had very strict ideas about what people could wear. Sometimes, after a very hot day, Uncle Tee would drive us all down to Lake Couchiching for a swim, but before we could get into the truck, we had to pass Grandma's inspection. She allowed no bathing suits, or shorts, or even long pants. We had to wear dresses over undershirts and bloomers. Once we were at the lake, we could take off our dresses and go in the water. At least the ride back to Rosewood was always pleasant because our soaking wet underthings kept us cool.

Other things were sinful. The main ones were playing cards and drinking alcohol. None of that bothered us but we noticed that when Uncle Ben and Aunt Ellen came up from Toronto for a visit, they always left their case of beer in their friend's car. That was their friend Mr. Trent, the one who drove them up. He was a bachelor.

We had prayer after every meal. The more I heard them talking to those different people the more I tried to get it straight. One day I just couldn't put it off any longer. My mother and Annie were doing the dishes, and I had finished my job of clearing the table. Grandma was still sitting in the dining room. She had pushed her chair back a little so the sun made a patch of light on her knitting. I got Puggy to stay there with me. I asked Grandma to tell me who those people were that she and Grandad prayed to. She didn't stop clicking her needles while she looked right at me through her little round glasses. She told me that

31

Jesus and Christ were the same person and that He was the son of God. When I asked her about the Lord, she said that was another name for God, but she said it was sometimes the name for Jesus too. "When you have trouble, you pray to the Lord for help. I hope you'll always be a good girl and pray."

Puggy was pulling at my dress from behind but I didn't want to give up yet. I told her to go out and play; I wanted to talk to Grandma some more.

I asked if these people ever came to visit and she said yes, but just in spirit; anyone who had faith could feel their presence. Everything about them was written down in the Bible. I asked her if they were something like Santa Claus. "No," she said. "People just made Santa Claus up to fool little children about Christmas."

"But I saw him," I said. "We all did. He came to our school and gave us presents."

She flipped her ball of wool to free some more yarn and went on knitting. "People just pretend," she said. "The real meaning of Christmas is the birth of baby Jesus. That's when he came into the world to save us all."

My mother came to the door, a dishcloth in her hand. "Bubba, you run along now. Don't be bothering Grandma."

I went out to look for Puggy, but all I could think of was how sorry I felt for poor Grandma. If she didn't believe in Santa, how was she ever going to get any presents at Christmas?

Maybe it was okay for Grandma to be the head of the house when it was just Grandad and Uncle Tee who lived with her. They were used to it. And it wasn't too bad for the three of us because we soon learned what we weren't supposed to do, and we kept away from her. Or for our father. He knew her from before he left home at the age of sixteen, so all her ways were familiar to him. Anyway, he was out working in the fields or at the barn with Uncle Tee most of the time. But it was different for our mother. Several times we heard our father ask her what was wrong and she said, "I think I just miss the mountains."

But one day when Annie and I came home from school everything was different. Our father was washing his hands at the sink. Our mother was sitting at the kitchen table with Puggy on her knees. I noticed for the first time that her stomach was big, because there was no room for Puggy in her lap. One thing different from usual was that our father was in the house at that time of day; it was different too because Grandad wasn't in the kitchen. I wanted to show him the picture I'd coloured in Art. It was a bluebird. Right away I said, "Where's my Grandad?"

Grandma and Grandad weren't going to use the kitchen any more, and they weren't going to eat with us either. They had moved all their food and cooking things into the little room next to their bedroom. Our father and Uncle Tee had set up an old cook stove for them in there. They would have to come to the kitchen to get water, but that was all. Uncle Tee ate with us mostly, but sometimes Grandma would get him to go in with them for a meal.

That happened in September, not long before Poppy was born. We spent as much time as we could around her when we weren't in school, playing with her and holding her and giving her a bottle, so I didn't miss Grandad all that much. Anyway, I could see him whenever he was outside.

33

Annie said that Grandma was mad about something we did, but I couldn't remember anything bad enough to make her move into the other rooms and not speak to anyone. Puggy told me it was something else, some bad things that Grandma said to our mother, but she didn't know what exactly. She was home with them all day and liked to play with her doll in the big cupboards in the dining room that you could walk into if you were short enough, but she said she couldn't hear things very well in there.

Things went on like that all winter, and all through the spring and the summer. Grandma talked to me only once in all that time, when she asked if she could use my paints. I ran upstairs and got them right away. It was a brand new paint box and it made me feel important that she asked me. Later, when she gave them back, she showed me what she'd needed them for. It was a round white plaster plaque with "JESUS ONLY" in raised letters. She had painted the letters. Before I put my paint box away again, I opened the lid. All the red was gone.

Aunts and uncles and cousins came to visit as before. Our mother cooked for them and the aunts helped. After a meal, they would go in to pray with our grandparents in their two rooms. Sometimes they would eat with them, but only one or two at a time.

Near the end of the next summer big trouble came. My mother sent me up to dust the furniture in our room. We all slept in the same bedroom, which had been the upstairs parlour when Grandad was growing up. He said his sisters used to sit up there, with a nice fire in the stove, and do their sewing and knitting and reading. It was really big so there was lots to dust. I heard my mother coming up the stairs. I was glad because I wanted her to see how much I had done already. But she hurried to the bed and lay down real hard on it. She was crying. I had never seen her cry before and I didn't know what to do. I started over to the bed but then my father was in the room. He didn't seem to see me at all. He sat beside her and spoke real low. " Come on, now, Kathleen. Don't let it bother you. You know what she's like. *We* know it isn't true and that's all that matters." He was stroking her hair. And then he said, a little louder, "Her and her goddam religion anyway. She's got no right to accuse you of something like that. That's the end. We're not going to stay here any longer."

My mother didn't say anything. She wasn't making any noise but her shoulders were moving up and down. My father looked up and saw me. "Away you go," he said. "I want to talk to your mother."

"But I haven't finished the dusting." I held up the oily cloth.

"Never mind the dusting. Away you go."

Aunt Jane and her two children, Angie and Mint, were up for a visit at the time, but there was no one in the kitchen or the dining room. I could hear voices in my grandparents' rooms. I found Annie and Puggy in the little back kitchen, a room off the kitchen with a slant roof, where the washing machine and the tubs were. Annie was crying and Puggy had a scared look on her face. I said, "What's the matter with Momma?"

So we moved to Uncle Court and Aunt Millie's farm at Hawkestone, nine miles on the other side of Orillia.

Annie blamed Mint because he went into the house and told Aunt Jane and Grandma what she had said to him. "All I said was that my last name isn't Cassidy. What's wrong about pretending my name is Brendan, what Momma's used to be? I just didn't want him to keep calling me 'Hopalong.'" My father blamed Grandma for listening to young kids and then accusing him and my mother of having a baby before they were married. "Our wedding was the first of August for God's sake, and the baby didn't come until the twenty-first of May!" Puggy didn't say much but I know she blamed Annie for saying such a thing at all, especially to Mint.

As for me, I blamed all those people Grandma prayed to. God and Jesus Christ and the Lord and the Holy Ghost. I blamed them because they shouldn't have let Grandma be the head of the house and say the kind of things she did and send us away to a place where our mother could get polio.

FIVE

BY THE TIME WE MOVED TO HAWKESTONE, WE HAD LIVED IN seven different places—five in B.C., one in Alberta, and then Rosewood Farm in Ontario. Those were just the ones I could remember. Before that we had lived on Big Bar Mountain in B.C. with our other grandparents. Both of them died between the time I was born and the time Puggy came along. Annie said she could remember them but we were never sure if she was just making it up to be important. Anyway, I was still seven when we moved to Uncle Court and Aunt Millie's house, and it was the eighth place. It was the eighth, and it was the ugliest. I really felt quite sorry for the house because it was so plain. But maybe it was just because the big white farmhouse at Rosewood had been by far the nicest place we'd ever lived, and the two were so different.

It was just as tall and it had as many rooms. Puggy and I counted them right away. The kitchen and the parlour made it even with our grandparents' kitchen and dining room, even if the parlour was small and was hardly ever used because it was just for very special times. And there were six bedrooms. Except that after we moved in there were only five because they gave one to us for a kitchen, a corner room downstairs. It had a stove and a few chairs. Our father had to make a wooden table for us to eat on. The house even had a back kitchen, with a stove for cooking on when the weather was hot, which was bigger than the one with the wash tubs at our grandparents'. So it wasn't the size of the two houses that made them so different.

The house seemed kind of skinny and held in and it didn't have any paint on it. The boards were grey except for some parts that had brown streaks, as though a dirty rain had stained them. And it was bare all around. There were no trees or bushes, no garden, and no porch, only the bare length of cement that ran along one side, where the kitchen door was. A step went down into the yard. There wasn't any fence between the barn and the house; the yard was all one big open space.

And the rooms, except for the kitchen and the parlour, seemed empty. The parlour was full—dining table and chairs, china cabinets, and shelves with ornaments and dried flowers—but its door was always closed. The other rooms had hardly any furniture. Two of the big rooms upstairs had none at all, except for a few boxes and one trunk.

Uncle Court was a lot like Grandad. He was tall and thin like him and he didn't have much hair, and he stood the same way, bent forward a little. But his face was very different. He was dark and didn't have a moustache, but it was more than that. Instead of having bright eyes and a smile always ready to be there, his face looked empty, like those rooms. Maybe it was from living there so long.

Aunt Millie was like the house too, but more like the outside of it. She was tall and real skinny. Her cotton dresses were pale as though they had been in the rain a long time, and her face was long and thin and wrinkled. Puggy and I tried to figure out how old she was. She had two boys, one a little older than Annie and one between Puggy and me, so we thought she couldn't be much older than our mother. But they were so different. We sometimes said we wouldn't mind having Uncle Tee for a dad, but we never once thought of anyone else for a mother. Another thing about Aunt Millie was her voice. If any of us had ever sounded anything like that our father would have said, "Stop whining!" But no one ever said that to her, especially not Uncle Court.

We felt kind of sorry for our two cousins, Harold and Lester, for getting parents like that, but it didn't bother us much because we were in our own part of the house. Our mother had brought some cotton material with her from the West and she soon had our downstairs room fixed up with bright curtains and a matching tablecloth. Aunt Millie offered her sewing machine but our mother said she was better at hand sewing and, anyway, she could look after the baby better that way. Our father wasn't home very much. He helped Uncle Court with the chores and the other farm work. At first they were getting in the wheat and oats and, later, they cut wood for the winter. They even cut some wood for a neighbour to make some money. The three of us went to the school up the road, about two and

39

a half miles beyond the store and the church. The school was different for us: for me and Annie because the teacher was a man, and for Puggy because she was just starting Grade One. On our first day, Harold and Lester seemed to feel very important to be showing us the way, and showing us which of the two doors was for girls. After that Harold didn't bother with us much. He'd run on home after school leaving us behind with Lester.

That was just after Labour Day, and then it was Hallowe'en. By early November the sign "POLIOMYELITIS" was on the gate, and then our mother was gone.

After the funeral, the aunts and uncles came to the farm to decide what was to be done. They talked among themselves as though we weren't there at all. One said it must be hardest for Annie because she was the oldest and understood best. Another said it was worse for the baby because she was so young and she wouldn't even remember her. Another said it was probably worst for Puggy because she was the one closest to her mother, being the baby all those five years before Poppy was born.

Aunt Ellen said that she and Uncle Ben would take the oldest one to live with them in Toronto. Aunt Mae and Uncle Vince said they would take the baby. Their farm was just down the road at the next concession. Aunt Ellen and Aunt Mae were two of our father's sisters. He didn't say much but he seemed to agree. That left Puggy and me.

Our grandparents did not come; Grandad was too sick. And Aunt Jane didn't either because she was at Rosewood looking after him. Uncle Tee came, and we all got to take turns sitting on his knee, even Poppy, but he wasn't married so he couldn't ask us to live with him. There was no other way. We were to stay on at Hawkestone with Uncle Court and Aunt Millie, and Harold and Lester.

At first, we just ate with them. We still had our corner room and our father took us in there, mostly just when it was bath time. He showed us how to stand up in the tub and put the towel behind us, holding one end with each hand, so we could dry our own backs. The room wasn't the same though because all our mother's things, even her new curtains and tablecloth, had been burned. Because of the polio germs.

Then our father had to take a steady job with the neighbour they'd been cutting wood for. The neighbour had a big farm across the creek, with lots of cows and pigs and chickens, and other hired men. He needed a lot of help to run such a big place. He even had a tractor and a hay baler. Our father ate with them and they let him stay in a bunkhouse with the other men.

After that we had to live with Aunt Millie and Uncle Court all the time. We already knew that Uncle Court was in the middle of our Dad's family, and that he had always been Grandma's favourite. We knew the older people made fun of him because he spent so much time with his team, currying and brushing them and braiding their manes and tails. They were Clydesdales. Queenie and Belle. But we didn't know very much about Aunt Millie, except that she was skinny, and wrinkled, and had a whiney voice. Right away, our corner room was made back into a bedroom for Uncle Court. They moved a bed and one chair down from upstairs. Aunt Millie had her own room with a narrow bed and a feather quilt, and a pillow stuffed into half of the

41

space of the open window. She needed fresh air, she said.

Puggy and I slept upstairs in the same room the four of us used before. The boys had a double bed in the room next to it. The door to the room at the top of the stairs, which had been our mother's and father's room, was kept closed. We didn't spend any more time upstairs than we had to because it was too cold. In the mornings Uncle Court and Harold did the milking and the feeding before breakfast. Puggy and I and Lester took our clothes down to the kitchen to get dressed for school. We had never seen anyone so slow as Lester, who would sit on a chair for a long time, one sock in his hand, with his eyes hardly open and dried spit all around the corners of his mouth. Aunt Millie would turn from the bread slices she was watching as they toasted on top of the stove and whine at him. "Lester dear, you keep moving. I can't get you off to school in time if you don't hurry up and get dressed." Then he would put one sock on and pick up the other.

She and Uncle Court and Puggy and I ate porridge every morning. Harold and Lester didn't like porridge. They had corn flakes and shredded wheat instead. We didn't like porridge either, but we thought it must be something the same as the way Puggy and I got a penny each for collection at Sunday school and they got ten cents. We knew it was because we weren't their own kids. We didn't like porridge, and especially we didn't like having to clean the sticky pot. She kept it soaking all day for when we got home from school.

One day when we had just finished the pot—Puggy was drying it and I was dumping the water with all the porridge pieces into the pail they kept for the chickens—

we heard a thump behind us. There was aunt Millie on the floor. She had fallen and was lying all crooked on her side. Her head was twisted around and her mouth was open. Her eyes were opening and shutting and she was moaning. I told Puggy to run and get Uncle Court, who was splitting wood at the back of the house. I knew you were supposed to throw water on people who fainted, but I didn't want to take time to go to the back kitchen for the pail of drinking water so I moved the chicken pail over beside her and dipped my hand in and sloshed water on her face. Bits of porridge stuck to her forehead and cheek. She opened her eyes wide, then closed them tight. When Uncle Court came in, I pushed the pail back out of the way.

He stooped down, got his hands under her, and lifted her up. Puggy and I stood at her bedroom door as he put her on the bed. Her eyes were open. She moved her arms around as though she was trying to catch onto something at the side of the bed. "Lester, Lester," she moaned.

"Not this again," Uncle Court said. He stood up. "Go get Lester. I think he's in the barn with Harold. I'll get her a wet cloth."

Puggy whispered, "What's wrong with her?"

Uncle Court said, "She's anaemic."

They were both following me to the kitchen. "What's that mean?"

"Her blood's thin. She doesn't have enough of it."

When I came back with Lester, Uncle Court took him by the hand and led him to the bedroom. He shut the door behind him and motioned to us to move back. "It's always Lester she wants," he said. "Never me, or even Harold. Whatever good she thinks it does calling for a puny boy like him, I don't know."

43

Since coming to live there, we had noticed some terrible smells in the house. One was from the towel by the kitchen door, which hung down from its roller low enough for us to dry our faces on. The material was rough and hard and had stripes of red and blue so faded into the yellow-brown of the part that wasn't striped that you could hardly see them. I hated to put my face into that roughness and that smell. It was like a turnip gone rotten all mixed up with sour milk. Another bad smell came from behind the stove. Puggy and I looked in there and saw a pail full of blood with some cloth things floating in it. It wasn't always there. Just for a while every few weeks. Puggy said maybe it was to help Aunt Millie because she didn't have enough blood, but I said, "I don't think so, because it's mixed with water. And has rags in it." It was a heavy smell, like something metal rusting in the rain.

In the middle of December, Aunt Ellen and Uncle Ben sent Annie back. She did something they didn't like. No one knew for sure what it was and Annie said she didn't know either. She brought a brown jar of medicine with her, something Aunt Ellen made her take. Aunt Ellen was a nurse and she knew what was good for everybody, especially children. Annie made sure to take it every evening right after supper. She put the spoon in and it came up full of sticky brown stuff. It smelled bad, like rotten fish. She said it was cod liver oil to give her Vitamin D because there wasn't enough sun in the winter.

All the time Annie was in Toronto, Puggy and I had to do the supper dishes. I washed them and she dried. The water was always greasy because we couldn't use any soap. That was so the dishwater could go in the pigswill pail and the chicken pail. Now Aunt Millie said Annie was to wash them and the two of us could dry, but Annie couldn't keep ahead of us both and in between drying plates or cups one of us would give her a little poke from behind. She would turn around fast, very mad, and when she saw us laughing she would look even madder, but turn back without saying anything.

Christmas was coming and we had a concert at school and another one at the church for all the Sunday School classes. Santa Claus came to them both but he wasn't the same as the one I'd seen in Grade One so I didn't really believe in him any more. He didn't bring any presents. A few weeks before, we all had to draw names. The boy who got my name at school gave me a little silver penknife and the girl who got my name at Sunday School gave me a book about Jacob and his brother Esau. It had pictures.

Annie said she had a secret about what she was getting for Christmas. But it wasn't long before she had to tell. Aunt Ellen and Uncle Ben had told her they would be sending up a doll for her. About the same time, Aunt Millie said that we would be getting presents. She said they were the same for the three of us except that Annie's was bigger. She didn't know the secret about the doll so we didn't say anything.

Christmas morning each of us woke up to see one of our long brown stockings hung at the end of the bed. Only the foot part was full. There were hard candies, and peanuts in their shells, and a tangerine.

Our father came over that day for Christmas dinner. We ate in the parlour. In the corner by the window there was a tree that didn't have very many branches, but the branches

45

had red and green paper chains and some tinsel on them. The plates weren't the plain ones from the kitchen; they were covered with flowers. After we finished eating Aunt Millie told us and the boys to go play somewhere while she did the washing up. Puggy thought it was because of the flowery dishes, but I thought it might have been because our father was there.

He and Uncle Court stayed at the table talking. I looked in once on my way past. Our father's head was bent down, his elbows on his knees. Uncle Court was rolling a cigarette. I couldn't hear anything they were saying.

And then it was time to open the gifts. The boys ripped the wrapping off their boxes. High-top, lace-up boots for Harold and a lacrosse stick. Skates for Lester and a dump truck. Uncle Court gave Aunt Millie two checkered tea towels and his present from her was a pair of work gloves. Annie unwrapped her doll and held its hands so it could stand on her knees. Its blue eyes opened and closed, and it had a frilly blue dress that poked out all around to show its matching bloomers.

Puggy and I sat with our presents in our laps. They were too small and too square to be dolls. Our father nudged us both. "Go ahead. Open them." We looked at each other and started together. First the red ribbon, then the green tissue paper. Something solid and black. We dropped the paper to the floor.

"They're not the same as Annie's." Afterward, Puggy said she just couldn't help saying that.

"Yes they are," Aunt Millie said. "See? Here's Annie's." And she held out a square parcel wrapped in red tissue with a green ribbon.

Annie took it and, holding it on top of the doll in her lap, undid the paper. It was the same as ours, only bigger and fancier. Three black Bibles.

Puggy didn't cry, not until we were in bed. We had gone up the stairs in the dark. Annie had her doll under the covers in the other bed, but we had left our Bibles on the windowsill in the parlour. I heard Puggy make a little sniffle, and her arm came slowly across my chest. I said, "Let's pretend we got dolls."

She shifted her arm a bit, I think to wipe her nose on the sheet. "Daddy didn't get *any* present," she said.

SIX

BEFORE WE LEFT OUR LAST PLACE IN B. C., WE HAD NEVER SEEN a town. We lived on a crick called Big Bar Crick which ran into a big river, the Fraser, and the closest place to our home was Jesmond. It was not a town; it was just a house, but part of the house was a store, and part of the store was a post office. There was a gas pump outside. That house was where the Colemans lived and they ran the store and the post office and sold gas. Our teacher, Miss McCleery, boarded with them, and their two girls went to school with us. The school was about halfway between their place and ours; it was a log cabin, just one room with a porch made of boards along the front. That's where Annie and I started Grade One when she was seven and I was five. Until then there was no teacher. That's why Annie had to wait so long to start school. She was real mad that we were in the same grade.

The day we left, Annie and I knew what an important

time it was. Maybe not Puggy, who was only four and a half. Mr. Boyd came for us in his car. Our parents put our suitcases and coats, and a box full of food for the train, in the trunk, and said goodbye to the people who were moving in. As we drove out of the yard, Annie and I shouted goodbye to the house, goodbye to the barn, and to the team and the three cows, and to the few hens that were scratching in the dirt at the side of the lane. And goodbye to the crick and the trees, and then to the gateway. The gateway was one of my favourite things. The poles went up on both sides and joined high up to a pole that went across. It was like a big doorway into the ranch, but now we were going out the door and leaving it behind. Then along the bumpy road it was goodbye to the schoolhouse, goodbye to Colemans' place, to the store and the post office.

After that there was nothing familiar left, so we quit saying goodbye. Our mother was in the back seat with us. She had Puggy in her lap. When we came to where there were trees on both sides of the road, she bent forward and looked up out of the window. She didn't speak very loud, but I heard her; she said, "And goodbye to you, my mountains."

Ashcroft, where we waited to get on the train, was a town but it didn't really count because it was at night and everything was dark. My mother said it was the town where I was born. She said Annie was born on Big Bar Mountain where our Grandaddy and Grandma lived, and Puggy was born in Oregon, but Ashcroft was my town. I wished the train wouldn't come until morning so I could see it.

There must have been lots of towns that we saw from the train but I don't remember them, only Edson in Alberta.

49

That's where we stayed for a few months with Uncle Phil and Aunt Carrie. He was our father's oldest brother. They had two boys, one just younger than me and the other still a baby. We had to be quiet a lot of the time because Uncle Phil worked on the CNR and slept in the daytime. I wondered at all the houses so close together and at all the people, but everybody said Edson was a very small town. Annie and I went to school in Edson but not for long. For some reason we had to stop. Maybe because it wasn't our province. Anyway, Aunt Carrie gave us lessons at home. She had been a teacher in Ontario before she and Uncle Phil got married so she knew how to do it. She said it would give us a head start because she was using the old Ontario school books.

Orillia, in Ontario, was bigger but we didn't see much of it. When we arrived, Uncle Tee met us at the train and took us right out to Rosewood Farm. Any time we did go to town it was always to the same places, the grocery store and the big market where the farmers brought all their vegetables and things to sell on Saturdays. We went back and forth to school, which was three miles from Rosewood in the other direction, and the rest of the time we stayed around the place. But there were lots of visitors. There always seemed to be people from one or the other of the Pentecostal churches, people either from Orillia or from Barrie. They sat at the dining-room table a lot and when they were finished eating they would get down on their knees with our grandparents. They didn't just listen. They said prayers out loud. One old man from Toronto came every summer for weeks at a time. He was a tailor. He always brought boxes full of suit samples for our grandmother, which she sewed together to make quilts.

But mostly, the visitors were relatives—aunts and uncles and cousins. Aunt Ellen and Uncle Ben came quite often. Their friend Russell (we had to call him Mr. Trent) drove them up from Toronto in his car. If they were staying for a week or so, he would drive back home again and then come for them when they were ready. When they came for their long visit the second summer we were there—but before Grandma and Grandad stopped eating with us—they had a baby. We had heard when she was born, about six months after Poppy, but that was the first time we saw her. They called her Allison. She wasn't good all the time and smiling the way Poppy was but it was fun for us to watch all the special things Aunt Ellen did for her, like boiling her bottles to kill the germs, and mixing pablum fresh for every meal, and squeezing oranges so she had fresh juice all the time. Aunt Ellen was a nurse so we knew those were all the right things to do. Poppy was still getting milk from our mother but she ate food too. She liked to have the food the rest of us were eating. We just mashed it up for her.

Uncle Ben used to go out in the fields or to the barn to help Uncle Tee and our father with some of the work. Uncle Tee told him not to work, to enjoy his holidays, but Uncle Ben said that doing farm work was how he enjoyed his vacation; it was different from reading gas meters in the city. But that summer he stayed in the house a lot. They used the little bedroom downstairs next to our grandparents' big one, and he was in there most of the time. Aunt Ellen said he was sick with something he'd had for quite a few years, and that was how they met. He was a patient in the hospital where Aunt Ellen was a nurse. They

51

thought he had been getting better but now he was worse again.

The first time Puggy and I heard him we were so scared we ran into the house to our mother. We had been making mud pies out in the side garden, on the wooden cover over the steps that went down into the cellar, just under the bedroom window. We were pretending to be witches and were just putting in the last of the poison berries, three in each of the pies that we'd set out in the sun to bake. We heard such a sudden, high-pitched scream that I dropped the tin I was holding and the last of the berries rolled in red lines down the wood of the cover. Puggy jumped, knocking over the last two pies in the row. We heard shorter, even louder screams. It sounded like a pig getting killed. We were never allowed to watch, but we could always hear the terrible squeals coming from the back of the barn when pigs were killed. These noises weren't from the barn, though; they came from the window over our heads, from the little bedroom.

In the kitchen, our mother shushed us and wiped the tears from Puggy's face. She said Uncle Ben was having an attack and that Aunt Ellen was looking after him. She said he was passing kidney stones. When we asked what that meant, she said some little stones had grown inside him and now they had to come out. We wanted to know where they were growing and where they were coming out and I thought she was about to tell us but there was another terrible scream, long and drawn out, and she just put her hands at our backs and pushed us toward the door. She said, "Go out to the barn now. You can play out there. I don't want you to have to hear this."

Puggy said, "Is it going to make him die?"

And our mother said, "No, but it's terrible pain. Aunt Ellen is doing everything she can to look after him. Away you go now."

There were more attacks after that, one nearly every day, but when we heard them start we would go out to the barn, maybe to look for hidden hens' nests, or down the road to where we were sure to find some frogs in the ditch, because we knew our mother didn't want us to hear them. Annie hadn't been with us that first day because she was visiting Mrs. Harvey at the next farm. After that when an attack started, she said she wouldn't go some place else with us because she wanted to be a nurse when she grew up so she should stay and listen.

A few days before it was time for them to go back to Toronto, the attacks stopped. I heard Aunt Ellen telling Grandma that Uncle Ben must have passed all the stones. I still wondered where they came out, and what Aunt Ellen did with them once they were out, but I didn't ask any more questions because I had something else to think about. Aunt Ellen and Uncle Ben told my mother they wanted to take me to the city with them for a visit. I didn't know what a city was, so they said it was like a town only way, way bigger. They said Toronto had traffic lights and street cars and thousands and thousands of stores and thousands and thousands of people. I couldn't imagine a place like that.

I don't think I even wondered why they wanted me instead of Annie. Of course Puggy and Poppy were too young to go away. I was too excited to think about anything except that I was the one to go. I think it was more Aunt

53

Ellen's idea than Uncle Ben's. He said, "We can't take her looking like that." His eyes moved away from my face and down my dress. It was dirty and my sleeve was torn and the seam at the waist was partly undone. He looked at my shoes, shaking his head. They were scuffed, one lace was missing, and the other was knotted up short. "We'll have to get her a whole new outfit," he said.

Once in a while we got new clothes, Annie and Puggy and I, from the catalogue. But I had never had new clothes from an actual store. That's where they took me. They asked my mother to look after Allison and got Uncle Tee to take us to town. While he went to do something else, they took me to a real store. I had to go into a little room and take my dress off. The one they picked out was white. The lady said it was piqué and showed us the fine lines in it, like little ribs. The vest and belt were the same material but dark blue. Aunt Ellen told me to take my bloomers off too because they made the new dress look bulky. Then Uncle Ben asked the lady if she sold underpants there as well, and they bought me two pair, white too, and very thin, and short. "What about socks?" he said. And they got me two pair, one white and one blue. Everything was nice, but it felt comfortable to get back into my old dress and put on my bloomers again.

After that we went to another store where a man sat down in front of me with a metal thing with marks on it. He took off my shoe and Uncle Ben opened the paper bag from the other store and handed him the blue socks. Once I had them on, the shoe man measured my foot, then went to the back of the store. Uncle Ben called after him: "Black ones would be best. Maybe patent leather?" Aunt Ellen let

54

me keep them on, my new shiny black shoes and my blue socks.

When we got home and went into the kitchen, they showed everybody all my new things; I thought nothing could ever spoil how I felt, even when Annie pinched my arm real hard when nobody was looking, and said, "You think you're so smart. Wait till you get down there and he starts screaming. Then where'll you go? You're such a scaredy cat."

My mother folded the dress and the other things and put them back in the bag. She handed it to me and smiled. "You'd better take these upstairs. You can put them in the bottom drawer for now. You're going to look real nice for the city."

Hugging the parcel to my chest, I went into the dining-room on my way to the stairs. Puggy was beside me. "I want to come too," she said.

Behind us I heard Uncle Ben's voice. "She didn't even say thank you. Can you imagine that? We bought her all those clothes and she didn't even thank us."

Then I heard my mother say something, but it was just a murmur, and Aunt Ellen said something too low to hear. Uncle Ben said, even louder than before, "We take her in and get her a whole new outfit and do we get any thanks? Not a word!"

I walked slowly through the dining room. The parcel felt heavier than before. Clothes and thank you's. I hadn't thought of them together before. We never had to say thank you for clothes from the catalogue. Maybe store-bought things were different. Suddenly I felt afraid about going to a big city.

At the bottom of the stairs, Puggy was pushing at me from behind. "Come on, hurry up! I want to try everything on!"

SEVEN

IT TOOK A LONG TIME TO GET TO THE CITY BECAUSE THE HIGHWAY was full of cars. When we got to the top of a hill, we could see long lines of cars all the way down to the bottom and all the way up the other side to the top of the next hill. One whole line was going to Toronto like us, another was coming the other way. Mr. Trent kept saying, "Bumper to bumper. In heat like this. Bumper to bumper. Can you believe it?" It was easy for me to believe because I could see it, but I was worried because when he talked he looked at Uncle Ben or back over his shoulder at Aunt Ellen, and I was sure he was going to drive off the road. There were a lot of cars off the road already. Most of them had hoods up with steam coming out. Some were up on jacks and men were changing tires.

The baby cried most of the time. Once in a while Aunt Ellen handed her to me and I bounced her a little the way I did with Poppy at home, but it didn't help. Her face was awfully red. I thought it was from crying, but Aunt Ellen said it was heat rash.

Aunt Ellen didn't talk to me very much while we were driving along, I think because she was worried about Allie. But she did say that she was going to call me Ginnie. She thought Bubba was too babyish for me, and Virginnia was too grown up. She said maybe Ginnie could be my city name. Mr. Trent kept muttering, "Bumper to bumper, all the way to the city. Jesus, I hope we don't get a flat."

The place Aunt Ellen and Uncle Ben lived was called a flat. It was like a house except that when you went through the door, you went up some steep stairs and ended up in the living room. It was dark when we got there but it had electric lights, so we didn't have to look around for a lamp. The only electric lights I had seen before were at Uncle Phil's place in Alberta.

Uncle Ben and Mr. Trent set the suitcases down beside the chesterfield. Uncle Ben said, "Come on, Russ. I'll get you a beer." I wondered what Grandma would say.

Both went into the kitchen. I could hear Mr. Trent say, "I could sure use a shot in the arm after a drive like that. Can you believe it?"

Aunt Ellen told me to come with her while she took the baby into the bedroom and put her in her crib. At the door, she switched on the light. "See if you can get her to stop crying. I'll change her and feed her as soon as I get all her things out of the suitcase. Then I'll make up a bed for you on the chesterfield so you can get back to sleep. Wasn't that an awfully long trip?"

I let Allie suck on my finger. My mother always told me to make sure my finger was clean before I put it in Poppy's mouth, but I didn't know where to wash my hands so I just wiped them on the bedspread. Anyway, it made Allie stop crying. She sucked real hard and jerked her hands back and forth. They didn't look like hands. They were just tiny pink balls.

I knew I was in the city but it didn't seem very big right then. I was sorry that I had gone to sleep in the car because after coming all that way I had missed seeing how big it was.

Before I went to bed, I used the bathroom. I had never seen a toilet inside a house before. Aunt Ellen showed me how to flush it when I was finished, but I already knew because of the toilet on the train. There were only sheets and a pillow for me on the chesterfield because it was too hot for a blanket.

I went to sleep fast but a screechy noise woke me up. At first I thought it might be Uncle Ben having an attack, but it wasn't coming from the bedroom. Actually, there were quite a lot of noises—the screechy one, then a crackling or sizzling sound like a bonfire when it really gets going, and in behind it all some sort of motor rumbling. It would stop for a while then start again. Screech, crackle, sizzle, rumble. I wondered how any one could sleep in the city if that was what happened every night, but I got used to it after a while and went back to sleep.

When I woke up in the morning, I thought it was too early. There were no windows in the living room and only a little light was coming through from the one in the kitchen, but it was light enough to get dressed by. The kitchen had a table and three chairs and a highchair and cupboards and a sink. There was no water bucket; there were taps instead.

Through the glass in the kitchen door I could see stairs going down the outside. They ended in a little patch of ground with a low fence around it. When Uncle Ben came into the kitchen and saw me looking out, he explained that that was their garden down there. There was another garden beside it and another set of stairs going up to the flat next door, which was on the other side of the wall in the living room; both flats were over a big store belonging to an Italian family, which sold mostly fruit and vegetables but ice cream too. He said he would take me down to get some when he got home from work and maybe I could learn Italian while I was there.

The noises I heard in the night were still there but muffled. An extra loud screech made me jerk my head and Uncle Ben laughed at me. "I guess you're not used to all the traffic noises, are you? That's just the streetcars going in and out of the roundabout. We're at the north end of the line. The terminal's just across Yonge Street from our front door. When we go for ice cream we'll go across and have a look." So I had lots of things to think about all day—finding out what streetcars looked like, learning Italian, and getting ice cream. I had had ice cream once before, when Mrs. Merrick at the next ranch made some in a little metal machine and gave Annie and Puggy and me a bowl each.

The day was mostly full of Allie crying. Aunt Ellen kept busy trying to get her to stop. She'd say, "She must need changing," or "I guess she's hungry," or "I wonder if she's got gas; that can be painful, you know." She let me help her because she knew I was used to looking after Poppy. After she changed Allie and fed her and she was still crying, Aunt

Ellen put her upright against her shoulder and walked her back and forth patting her back. But she didn't stop. Her face was red and twisted, and her little red fists kept jabbing at the air. When none of those things worked, Aunt Ellen said, "She probably needs to sleep. I'll try putting her down for a bit." She took her into the bedroom and shut the door. The sounds were muffled but they didn't stop. Before long the crying got louder and louder. I didn't know a baby could cry so much, or so loud, or so long. Aunt Ellen came out and closed the door behind her. She sat down on the chesterfield beside me but she didn't say anything. She just let her head fall back against the cushion and stared at the ceiling. The way Allie was crying then, I thought she might choke, but finally she did get a little quieter.

That was how the whole day went. Changing. Feeding. Walking. Going into the bedroom. Allie's terrible crying. Over and over. The times they were in the bedroom I would go to the kitchen window, look out at the little square of garden and count the steps going up into the next apartment. Seventeen. If I counted the ground as one, and the porch at the top as one, there were nineteen.

I had counted again up to eleven when a loud, jangling noise, closer than Allie's crying, stopped me. The telephone. I expected Aunt Ellen to come out and answer it but she didn't and it kept on ringing. I looked at the door. She couldn't hear it. I didn't know what to.

I ran to the door and opened it. I saw Aunt Ellen on the bed, her face turned away from me. She had the baby on her knee, her hand in mid air. It came down hard with a slap, followed immediately with another, and another. Then both her hands grabbed up the bundle of noise, and shook it and shook it; the pink baby blanket slid to the floor, and Allie's crying was screams and chokes. I stumbled backwards and shut the door. The telephone had stopped ringing.

Long before Uncle Ben got home from work, I had forgotten all about the streetcars and the traffic lights, even the ice cream. He brought me a big ball with red and white patterns that looked like clouds. He said I could play with it on the porch outside the kitchen door, but maybe not until morning because he wanted to take me over to the roundabout. I put it on the chesterfield beside my pillow and folded sheets and said, "Thank you. It's very nice."

Aunt Ellen came out of the bedroom and hugged Uncle Ben. "If you're going to take her out, you might as well take the baby too. She's been giving us a terrible time today." She looked at me and gave a kind of sigh, as though she meant to let him know that she and I had suffered together. " She's quieted down a bit now. Maybe some fresh air will put her to sleep."

It was noisy on the street. Uncle Ben told me to hold onto the side of the baby carriage. And from there, I couldn't tell whether Allie was still crying or not. "We'll cross at the traffic light," he said. At the corner, he stopped. I wondered how we could ever get across with so many cars going by fast. He pointed up at a big red light. "When it turns green, we can cross over." So that was what traffic lights were. I thought they might be big lights that moved along with the traffic, maybe just at night. When the light turned green, all the cars stopped and we walked in front of them. I held on tight.

The streetcars were different from what I thought they'd

be too. They were more like the coaches on a train. Or like big buses. One was stopped just inside the roundabout. It was red and yellow and had windows all along the sides; it had a long pole out the back that reached up to black wires which ran in a big circle above. People were running toward it. Suddenly doors opened up, some at the front and some at the middle, with a loud swishing sound. People hurried to get on. Then the doors closed. Once the streetcar started off, I could tell what had made all the noises I'd heard in the night. The screeches came from the wheels starting up on the tracks. The crackles and sizzles came from the long pole that made sparks where it connected with the black wire. And the rumbling was from the whole streetcar when it got going.

When we got back across the street and into the store below the flat, Uncle Ben wheeled the buggy up to the long counter. I looked in at Allie. She was asleep. Her face was still red but her hands had stopped moving. Uncle Ben was saying, "I'd like a cone for the little girl." And the lady said, real clear, so we could both understand her, "What flavour?" How did they expect me to learn Italian if she spoke English the same as us?

There were three flavours. Chocolate, strawberry, and vanilla. I had the strawberry. For once that day, something was way better than I had thought it would be.

The next day was about the same. Allie cried all the time. Aunt Ellen kept trying everything she could to make her stop. Finally she took her into the bedroom and closed the door. At least I had my ball. So I wouldn't have to listen to the terrible choking sounds, I took it out on the porch and bounced it against the wall of the kitchen the way

Uncle Ben told me to. When I heard Aunt Ellen back in the living room, I would go in again. Late in the afternoon, I was bouncing it extra hard because the baby's crying was so loud I couldn't blot it out any other way. On one of the high bounces, the ball went over the railing, hit the side of the stairs on the way down, jumped sideways, and went into the garden next door. It rolled a little way and stopped under some big cabbage leaves. I could see bits of the red cloud pattern showing through. Uncle Ben had told me not to go down the stairs. They were dangerously steep, he said. But even if I did , the fence was too high for me to get over and, anyway, I would be afraid to go into somebody else's garden. I stayed out there until I heard the bedroom door opening.

When Uncle Ben came home, he took me down to the store for ice cream again. There were two boys sitting by a tub of water washing tomatoes, drying them and putting them into baskets. One was about as old as Annie and the other one was older. They were yelling at each other across the tub but I couldn't understand one single word. Uncle Ben said, "Ginnie, the lady wants to know what flavour today."

I said, "Chocolate." He bent his head down and gave me an angry look, so I was real quick to say, "Please."

The chocolate tasted good but I couldn't eat it, not more than a few licks. By the time we were back up the stairs, it was running down the sides of the cone and over my fingers. Aunt Ellen said, "Look at the mess you're making. You've got to eat it fast in this heat." She took me to the sink and wiped my hands with the dishcloth. Then she wiped off the cone and handed it back.

I said, "I don't want any more."

Uncle Ben was beside us then. He had Allie up against his shoulder. Her crying was just low sobs and she had one fist pushed against her mouth. "You don't want your ice cream? Why didn't you say so in the first place?" He moved me ahead of him with his knees as he walked toward the chesterfield. "You sit right down here and eat it." I raised the cone to my mouth and pretended to lick it. "I buy you a treat and that's all the thanks I get."

In a few moments the ice cream was running down my hand again. Aunt Ellen said, "Oh, Ben, she's got tears. You can't make her eat it." She took the cone and set it in the ashtray, then crouched down in front of me. I could feel lots more tears coming so I lay down sideways and turned my head into the pillow so she couldn't see my face. I felt her hand on my shoulder. "What's the matter, Ginnie? Aren't you feeling well?" There wasn't anything I could say to her, but her hand pressed against me and the way she sounded made me feel worse and I started to cry out loud.

Uncle Ben said, "Oh, for God's sake"; that made me think of Grandma again, and what she'd say about swearing. Right away I wanted my mother and my father and Annie and Puggy and our own baby. I cried even harder.

Aunt Ellen said, "There must be something wrong with her." She put her face close and whispered into my ear. "Come on, Ginnie. Tell Aunt Ellen what's the matter. Do you feel ill?" I shook my head. "Are you homesick then?" I shook my head again. She moved away a little and said out loud, "There's got to be some reason you're so upset. You'd better tell me so we can do something about it." When I

65

didn't say anything, she put her hand back on my shoulder and shook me. " I mean it! You tell me."

I knew I would have to say something, but there was no way to tell her the real thing. I opened my eyes a little. They felt stingy. She was looking at me in that same angry way Uncle Ben did. I moved my hands lower down and doubled over them. "My stomach hurts."

"Okay, Ben, that does it. I'm calling Dr. Anderson. We can't have her being sick while she's here with us."

"You know how much it's going to cost for a house call? We already got her all those clothes. This can't be anything serious."

"I've been wanting him to have a look at Allie anyway." Aunt Ellen got up and reached for the phone. "And it won't cost any more if he sees them both at the same time. He'll just charge for one call."

Uncle Ben said, "Whatever you think, but they've both stopped crying now."

The doctor was bald like Grandad and Uncle Ben, but he wasn't old like Grandad and he wasn't as young as Uncle Ben. He had a nice soft voice. "Show me exactly where it hurts." He pulled my dress up in front and pushed my underpants down a little way. He took my hand and moved it to my stomach. I couldn't think which would be the best spot, so I put it right in the middle. "Well, at least it's not her appendix," he said. He moved my hand away and put his own where it had been. He pressed hard on the spot. "Does that hurt?" It did hurt a little because he pressed so hard, so I nodded my head. "And does it hurt here?" He had moved his hand to the left. I nodded again. "What about here?" Now his hand was up a bit and to the right.

Again I nodded because I thought he would believe me more if it hurt in lots of places. "But mostly right here, is that correct?" He was pointing straight at my belly button and moving his finger in a kind of circle. I looked up at him. He was smiling, and his eyes looked twinkly like Grandad's. Then he winked.

He pulled the elastic into place, smoothed my dress down, and patted my shoulder. Then he turned around to Uncle Ben and Aunt Ellen. "There is some trouble," he said. "I think if I could talk to her alone for a bit I might be able to make a better diagnosis. Would you mind going into the bedroom?"

Once the door closed behind them he turned back to me. "Your stomach doesn't hurt at all, does it?" I was about to say that it truly did, but the way he was smiling I knew there was no use. So I shook my head. "What is it then, really? Why are you telling me it does?"

I was so surprised I didn't know what to say. I couldn't think of anything. Then I remembered about the ball. "Well, I lost my ball."

"That's nothing to play sick over, is it?"

"Uncle Ben bought it for me." I couldn't keep looking at him when I said the rest. "I don't want him to get mad."

"So." He made that one word very long and slow. "You are pretending to be sick because your uncle might get mad at you?" I nodded, still without looking at him.

He sat forward on the chesterfield, pulled me over so that I was standing between his knees. He put his hands on my shoulders. "Come on now. I want to tell you something. I'm a doctor, right?" I nodded. "Well, I had to study for years and years to become a doctor. One part of

67

my studies was to learn how to tell when my patients are just pretending to be sick. Do you understand that?"

Now I was looking right into his eyes. They were light blue and kind of watery. I nodded.

"And do you know what another part was?" I shook my head. "Another part was so I'd be able to tell when my patients aren't telling me the truth. I want you to think about that for a minute."

He took his hands off my shoulders and put them on his knees. "You look like a bright girl," he said, "but you're worrying your aunt and uncle, and goodness knows they have enough to worry about. So, right now, I want you to tell me the truth. Remember, I'll know if it's the truth or not. What is it that's bothering you so much?"

I felt I was in the corner of a fence, with no way through or over or back, just like a groundhog I had seen trying to get away from Uncle Tee's dog. So I had to say it. It came out like a whisper: "She hits the baby."

His head gave a little jerk and his eyes grew wider. "What? What did you say?"

I didn't want to make it any louder for fear they would hear it in the bedroom. I leaned closer to him, right beside one ear. "She hits Allie. She takes her in there and closes the door and hits her. And when she doesn't stop crying, she shakes her. She shakes her real hard." I started to cry again.

He reached for a kleenex and wiped my eyes, then put it in my hand. "Okay, you're a good girl. You've told me the truth. I can see that. You leave the rest up to me. I'm the doctor, remember." He moved me back, got up, and patted my shoulder. I dabbed the kleenex at my eyes and sat down

68

on a chair. He knocked softly on the bedroom door.

"Okay," he said, as Uncle Ben and Aunt Ellen came out. Neither was carrying the baby, and there was no sound coming from behind them. "Okay, okay," he said again. "I think we've located the trouble." I pressed the kleenex tight between my hands.

My aunt and uncle both looked at him, waiting. "Here's the trouble," he said. "She's got an upset stomach, all right. You said she wouldn't eat her ice cream? Well, I think maybe she's allergic to it. I'm going to leave this prescription with you." He took a pad out of his leather bag and leaned over the table. "It should relieve the symptoms for now. But I suggest that you get her home, back to the farm, as soon as you can." As he handed a slip of paper to Aunt Ellen, he said in a very quiet voice, as though I wasn't supposed to hear, "I think the main problem is just that she's a tad homesick."

He moved back over to me. With his back to the others, he raised my chin a bit with one finger. "Maybe this city life is a bit too much for you." Then he winked. It was a serious wink. His eyes seemed to have no twinkle left in them at all.

He picked up his leather bag. "Now," he said, moving toward the bedroom, "that baby girl of yours. I haven't checked her for a while, have I? Let's see if we can't get to the bottom of this crying you're telling me about."

He turned at the door to face Aunt Ellen. "And you too. I'd better have a look at you while I'm here. I'm guessing that you've let yourself get a little rundown." He put his hand on her shoulder. "You're a bright young nurse," he said, "so you've got to look after yourself. If you cave in,

69

who's going to take care of the rest of the family?"

They all went into the bedroom. I stuffed the wadded up kleenex into the pocket of my dress and slid off the chair. I thought I'd better go find out if I could still see my ball.

EIGHT

THE SUMMER AFTER OUR MOTHER DIED WE WERE STILL LIVING
at Hawkestone with Uncle Court and Aunt Millie, but
Uncle Tee came to get us in the red truck and took us
to Rosewood Farm so we could be there when our father
came back from the West. He was bringing our mother's
sister from Oregon who was to take all four of us, even the
baby, to the United States to live with her. Puggy and I
leaned on the sill of the kitchen window watching the road.
"It's a black car," I told her, "with a red stripe along each
side." She didn't remember Uncle Phil's car from the time
we lived in Edson. We didn't know how Aunt Mary got to
Alberta from Oregon but Uncle Phil was driving her and
our father all the way to Ontario. I said, "It's a long, long
way. Do you remember the time on the train?" But Puggy
said no, she didn't remember.

The car that turned into the laneway later that
afternoon was not a black one with red stripes. It was

maroon and, instead of being square and tall like the one I remembered, sloped down in back. I thought maybe it was someone else coming to visit. Then I saw Uncle Phil driving, and our father sitting beside him. We called down the cellarway to Annie who was helping our grandfather churn butter. "They're here! They're here!" She ran upstairs fast and we all dashed across the kitchen to the door. We stood together, the three of us, on the broad flat stone outside. Grandad came slowly up the steps inside.

After our mother died I had a lot of dreams about her, but I could never see her face. She was always walking away from me. When I was awake, even if I shut my eyes tight, I couldn't see what she looked like. Now here she was, getting out of the back of Uncle Phil's car, turning toward me; it was her face, as familiar as ever. Her hair was shorter and a little grey, and she had thick-rimmed glasses, but it was her face. I hadn't forgotten it at all. Puggy pulled her hand out of mine and ran toward the car: "It's Momma!"

Our father picked her up and gave her a kiss on the cheek. "Well, girls, here's your Aunt Mary," he said.

She didn't seem so much like our mother once we heard her name; she was just herself, our Aunt Mary. Grandma was visiting Aunt Jane in Barrie and I was glad. I thought maybe she didn't want to see Aunt Mary because she was ashamed of how she had treated our mother, but Uncle Tee said it was because of Angie's birthday. So we had Aunt Mary to ourselves for the few days she was there. She helped Grandad with the cooking and told us about Oregon. One night they were sitting around the table talking and Annie and I were washing dishes in the kitchen; Puggy went back and forth and told us what they said. They talked about "driving across the line" and "getting to Detroit" and wondered "if the kids would be allowed to stay in the States."

I must have been pretty big by then; I was over eight and a half, but Aunt Mary let me sit on her lap as much as I liked. Sometimes both Puggy and I sat on her knees at one time. Annie had to stand to one side, or behind her, but she usually left right away. Puggy and I stayed. We took turns running a comb through her hair. She had big waves on both sides and she told us how to fix them; we had to comb them down flat and then fluff them up so her hair spread out a bit at the ends. It caused little white speckles to fall onto her shoulders, which really showed up on the dark blue material of her dress. She gave us a little brush to sweep it off. She said she hadn't been able to wash her hair or take many baths since she left home. Puggy cleaned her glasses with a small piece of flannelette from a doll blanket that she kept in her pocket. Aunt Mary said she was used to having a bath nearly every day at home and it was difficult being in a place with no bathroom.

Oregon must be quite different from Ontario. It wasn't a province. They didn't have provinces across the border, they had states. That was why it was called the United States. When I asked her if Oregon had towns and a city like we had, she smiled a little and said yes, she lived in a town about the size of Orillia named Medford. The biggest city was Portland, but it wasn't as big as Toronto.

Once we were in Oregon living with her our lives would be very different. She said, "Uncle Dell can teach you how to play the fiddle. Your mother played the fiddle really well. Did you know that?" We didn't. One day when

73

we were peeling potatoes together I asked her if I had to get every bit of peel off, even around the eyes where it was hard to get at, and she said, "When you come to live with me, you won't have to be that particular, but you'd better do it while you're here." She said we wouldn't have to wear long stockings, or even long underwear in winter. She gave us names of different aunts and uncles and cousins we didn't know. There was a whole other family that was our mother's, some living in the next state, called California, but most in Oregon.

Aunt Mary helped us sort through our clothes. We didn't have much to begin with, but she said, "This sweater looks too small for any of you." "This dress is pretty worn out." "You'll all have to have new shoes when we get to Oregon anyway, so let's just take the ones you'll be wearing." When she was finished, there was only one small box.

When it was in the car, along with Aunt Mary's suitcase and our father's old valise, and we were ready to go, we had to wait for Aunt Mae and Uncle Vince to bring Poppy over from Hawkestone. She wasn't quite two years old yet; she didn't understand anything about going to another country, or to a state called Oregon.

While everyone was waiting, Puggy and I went to the barn to say good-bye to the animals. The cows and sheep were in the pasture somewhere so we couldn't include them. There were some young calves in pens though. They ran over when they saw us, thinking it was feeding time. The eight pigs were lying on their platform in one corner of their big enclosure. The floor all around them was mucky and wet, but the platform was clean and dry, and they were

74

all stretched out on the straw. A couple of them raised their heads and grunted when we looked over the low wall. The rest of them were asleep, one cheek deep in the straw and one ear flopped forward. Puggy said, "Their eyes are shut so tight, it looks like they don't have any eyes at all."

We stayed with the horses longest. Bette was in one stall with her young colt, Tony. We went in beside her and watched him bunt up and down under her belly. When he brought his head out, his lips were white with milk. They looked even whiter against the black of his face, just the way his whole body looked blacker against Bette's white side . Puggy asked me, "How come Tony is so black when his mom is so white?" I tried to explain the way Uncle Tee told me: they were Percherons, and with Percherons the foals are born black and then get lighter and lighter as they get older. I took her to see the older colt in the next stall and showed her that he was lighter already. His name was Bert. He was two years old, born just before we came on the train. We didn't go into the stall with him because he liked to bite; he'd even kick if we got behind him. Uncle Tee said it was because our father teased him when he was a colt, that first summer we were at Rosewood.

Puggy stood with one arm over Tony's neck. We were one on each side. We pressed our faces into the stubby hair of his mane, but only for a few seconds because he pulled away and ducked his head back under, where the milk was.

We heard Uncle Vince's car. He liked to toot the horn all the way up the lane. We ran out of the barn, calling as we ran: "Good-bye Bette and Tony and Bert." "Good-bye calves and pigs." "Good-bye sheep and cows, wherever

75

you are." "Good-bye hens and you old rooster. We don't have time to come in and see you." And then we were at the house. Uncle Vince was shaking hands with everybody, and Aunt Mae was just getting out of the car on the other side with Poppy in her arms; Poppy clung to a little plaid suitcase. When Aunt Mae set her down and went to the house, Poppy ran to us, but she didn't let go of the suitcase.

It was a very long way to Detroit. Sometimes Aunt Mary sat in back with us. When she did, Annie sat in front with Poppy on her knee. It was nice to lean against Aunt Mary and feel her arm around me. She had her other arm around Puggy. We stopped a few times to get gas for the car and go to the toilet. Aunt Mary had made up a big box of sandwiches, which were mostly tomato, so they got kind of soggy, but some were salmon with vinegar. There was chocolate cake too, and Uncle Tee had put in apples.

I was asleep by the time we got to the end of Lake Erie; Annie and Puggy and Poppy were asleep too. Our father shouted at us to wake up because we had come to the tunnel. It wasn't dark the way I thought it would be because it had lights all along both sides. But it was very, very long, so I went to sleep again right there under the river. When the car stopped, I woke up. Aunt Mary said we were in Detroit, in the United States.

We were beside a little stall with glass all around. The man inside told us to park by the big building and go inside. Our father took Puggy and me by the hand; Aunt Mary carried Poppy, and Annie walked beside her. There were tall counters everywhere, with people in lines in front and men in uniforms behind. When we stopped inside the door, one of the men beckoned us to come over to him. He talked to our father and then to Aunt Mary, and he kept looking at all of us with his finger raised and moving back and forth as though he was counting us over and over. It was noisy; I could hear their voices but I couldn't understand their words. Maybe I was just too sleepy.

I saw the man point off to one side; then, suddenly, a woman was standing next to us. She was short and fat like Grandma but she had on a uniform, dark blue like the men's. She picked Poppy off the counter where Aunt Mary had set her and put her hand on Annie's back, then on mine, to show us she wanted us to walk ahead of her. Puggy moved behind Aunt Mary but she had to come with us too. Our father bent down so we could hear him and he said, "It's okay. You go with the lady. She needs to examine you."

She took us through a door into a small room with nothing but a big table and a small chair. She put Poppy on the table and started to undress her. At the same time she said to us, "Take off your sweaters and dresses, and put them on the table. You can leave your panties on and your shoes." Puggy and I looked at each other and stood still, but when we saw Annie unbuttoning her sweater, we did the same. We all pulled our dresses off over our heads. Poppy was looking around the side of the blue uniform with a kind of scared face, but when she saw us undressing she started to laugh and pulled off one shoe and dropped it on the floor. That made us laugh too.

"Cut that out now," the woman said. "Put your clothes on the table." She left Poppy and came over to us. She pulled out the elastic of Annie's bloomers and looked down

77

inside. She did the same with me, and then with Puggy. She went back to Poppy and started putting on her dress and pullover. "Okay," she said, "You can put your clothes back on."

On the way back, the tunnel seemed shorter and not so well-lit. Aunt Mary sat in front with our father. They talked from time to time but we couldn't hear what they were saying. Annie wrapped Poppy in a blanket and let her lie across her legs and mine. Puggy leaned into me from the other side. We slept most of the way.

~

Grandad said, "Well, you're not going to be Yankees after all." He lifted each one of us up and made a loud kissing sound.

Aunt Mary said, "I can't believe they turned us down just because Dell doesn't have a steady job. I was really hoping to have the girls with us."

Our father didn't say anything at all.

They left a few days later. Aunt Mary made another big box of sandwiches and Uncle Tee put in apples. She hugged us, one after the other, and kissed us too, with tears in her eyes. Her glasses had specks on them.

We stayed in the yard watching the maroon car go down the road. Then it was over the hill and out of sight. Uncle Tee went back to the field to hoe potatoes. Annie picked Poppy up and went into the house with Grandad to help with supper. Puggy and I went to the barn.

We didn't say anything to the hens and the rooster as we went by. We didn't even look into the calf pen or the pig pen. We left lots of room as we passed behind Bert, where he was tied in his stall. The colt was a black mound in the straw beside his mother but he jumped up when we came in. Bette turned her head toward him and gave a little low nickering sound. We stood one on each side of him. He put his face up to mine and blew through his nostrils, then he nudged Puggy in the chest with his nose. She said, "We're back, Tony. They wouldn't let us stay in that other country." The colt jumped back a few steps, turned, and ducked his head in under the white belly. All we could hear were the sucking noises.

NINE

THE SECOND TIME AT HAWKESTONE WITH UNCLE COURT AND Aunt Millie it was different. Maybe we hadn't been there in the warm weather before, or maybe it was just that I was older. Nine. But there were more good things this time, at least outside the house.

Puggy and I wore only overalls—no blouses, or shoes, or even underpants. Behind the house, just to the side of the ramshackle hen coop, was a tall poplar tree with a swing in it, the rope tied under the wooden seat in two ragged knots. We could swing very, very high, especially if we got on together, Puggy sitting down and me standing up, so we could both pump. And there was a cool, clear creek, its waters bright where the sun hit it, but dark beneath the overhanging brush. We waded in with freshly-cut poles, dropped our lines and caught little wriggling fish: rainbows and chubs. At another place, where it ran through the lower fields, was a deeper spot. It was as though the water stopped for a while and turned around and took time to think about itself. We would take off our overalls and slide down the steep banks between the cattails and reeds into the clear water. As soon as our feet touched the bottom, the mud churned around us, almost to our waists.

Maybe best of all was Dolly, the little brown mare that Uncle Court let us ride whenever we wanted. All we had to do was climb into her manger, slip off her halter, put on the bridle, and step up onto her back. We usually got on together, Puggy in front. We backed her out of the stall, then rode her around the barnyard and down the lane to the lower fields. We could get off whenever we wanted by holding onto her mane and lowering ourselves to the ground. It was harder to get back up. We had to find a big rock, or a fencepost.

There were posts on both sides of the lane, with sagging wire between them. We noticed a hole, about halfway up one of the posts. We steered Dolly over to take a look. As we slid off, a bird flew out of the hole. It flew straight then dropped down to perch on the top wire. It was blue with orange on its chest. I couldn't see anything in the hole. I put my hand in and moved it down quite a way, down until I felt rough twigs and dry grass and small round warm shapes. Five. I brought one out, and held it for Puggy to see. Looking small in the middle of my hand, it was a pale blue egg.

When we told Aunt Millie about it, she said, "Oh, that's a bluebird! You shouldn't go near their nest. If you touch their eggs, they might never come back to sit on them and the young don't hatch out. They'll die in the shell. You wouldn't want that to happen, would you? They're such a pretty bird." We were careful after that, passing with Dolly on the far side of the lane, away from the post; we felt better when we saw birds still flying in and out of the hole.

Those were things away from the house. Inside, though, it was still the same dark, sad place: the same sour smells, the same whiny voices, the same empty rooms, especially the one at the top of the stairs where I had helped our mother to drink orange juice. I felt sorry for the house; it was so ugly, inside and out. But one day it became more interesting for me because of the starlings. I was sitting on the edge of the cement platform with Harold's little tabby in my lap. I liked to pet her and listen to her purr but I had to be careful not to let Harold catch me. He said she was his cat and nobody else was to touch her, but he didn't even have a name for her. If she were mine, I would call her Nancy, the name of a girl I liked at the school in Alberta. I wondered if I would ever have a cat all my own. She wasn't allowed in the house and nobody was allowed to feed her. If she got fed, they said, she wouldn't catch mice. She had kittens somewhere, probably in the barn. You could tell because her fur was sometimes wet and slicked down around the little knobs on her belly. She rubbed against my arm as I moved my hand from the top of her head, along her back, to the tip of her tail. Mixed with her purrs were other sounds, whirrs and chirps, that came from somewhere above me. I looked up and saw that the house, though it was ugly, was a nice place for birds.

The roof didn't come down far over the walls, which is one reason the house looked so plain. At the very top, under the eaves, I saw some movement. Birds darted in and out, chattering as they flew. They were completely black, and the ones that flew in were carrying long pieces of dry grass or straw or string. They were making nests right there. That should make the poor old house feel better. I watched them every day, and every day there seemed to be more birds. They used the whole length of wall, under the roof, on all four sides of the house. I didn't tell anybody, not even Puggy. It was a nice secret to have.

Harold was two years older than me, and Lester was between Puggy and me, but they didn't play with us. They didn't play with each other either. Harold had to do a lot of work, but when he wasn't cleaning out the cow barn or doing the milking or splitting wood, he would grab his lacrosse stick and go out to the long platform at the side of the house and flip the ball up off the cement, bounce it against the wall, and catch it in the net. It was different for Lester, who didn't have to do any work, not even when Uncle Court told him to, because Aunt Millie wouldn't let him. She said he wasn't over whooping cough yet; anyway, he was too young. He did cough a lot but usually just when she could hear him. When we were out in the yard together, he didn't cough at all. He threw rocks at me without saying anything, so I didn't know why he wanted to hurt me. He wasn't that way with Puggy.

I learned to run fast that summer just to keep away from the stones. I also learned to whistle and to climb trees. At first I could make notes only by blowing out; it took a lot of practice before I could make them by sucking in as well, but before it was time to go back to school, I could whistle a whole tune. The song I practised most was "Cowboy Jack," the one about a cowboy "out on the lonely prairie, where the skies are always blue." Our mother used

83

to sing it. And I practised climbing the big poplar with the swing in it. If I carried the old wooden box over from the henhouse and stood on it, I could reach one of the bottom branches, then I could pull myself up, one branch at a time. I liked to disappear into the leaves. No one knew I was there, not even Uncle Court when he came and stood at the door of the woodshed and undid the buttons at the front of his pants and peed on the ground. I decided I wanted to get good at whistling and climbing. They had nothing to do with being chased by Lester.

When Aunt Millie used the strap on us I tried to shut out the sting by whistling to myself. She strapped us when Puggy and I came home from school with our long stockings rolled down to our ankles because it felt good to have bare legs on a hot afternoon. We still hurt when it was time to go to bed. When Puggy took off her dress I could see the marks on her back, long and red and raised up from the rest of her skin. I had the same marks on me; I could feel the shape of their stinging.

Another time was over onions. Aunt Millie had told me to bring her eight or ten from the garden. I pulled them up, but they were so big and the tops were so long that I got a gunny sack from the root cellar to carry them back to the house. She grabbed the sack from me. "What have you done? You stupid girl!" She reached for the strap. Between whacks on my back and on my legs she shouted: "I tell her to go get me green onions." Whack! "A few little green onions for the fried potatoes. And what does she do?" Whack! Whack! "She pulls up the Spanish onions. Now what'll we do for onions this winter?" Whack! Whack!

When we got ready for bed, Puggy touched the stripes

of pain softly with her cool fingers. "You'll have to sleep on your stomach again," she said.

With my face pressed sideways on the pillow I couldn't whistle, so I shut my eyes and pretended I was high up in a tree.

No matter how often she strapped us or how much it hurt, though, we knew it was much worse for Harold. We didn't know why they hit him so much. Sometimes it happened in the barn. We could hear him hollering and crying, so we knew Uncle Court was hurting him. Sometimes Aunt Millie caught hold of him in the house and called for Uncle Court to come hit him. Uncle Court always came. He didn't seem to need a reason. He would punch Harold all over on the head and body while Aunt Millie held him and kept shouting, "Give him another one, Court!" and "Hit him harder!" and "Give it to him again!" Puggy and I stood and watched. We didn't want to, we just did. We both cried but didn't move away. Lester watched too, but he didn't cry.

Before long, my secret in the ledges above the walls wasn't a secret any more. Even if no one had noticed the birds constantly flying in and out or their loud quarreling, the white streaks of their droppings down the weathered boards were there for everyone to see. They reminded me of the whitewash on my Grandma's henhouse. Aunt Millie complained to Uncle Court about them until one Saturday morning when we were ready to go to town she couldn't stand it any more. The old Ford truck was loaded with boxes of vegetables for market (from the few such as beets, turnips, potatoes, and carrots that were still in the root cellar), Lester was already on the seat in the middle of the cab, Harold and Puggy and I were on the old car seat beside the vegetables in back, and Uncle Court was just getting in behind the wheel.

She stopped in the doorway and looked up at the bird droppings. "Court, these starlings have to go. Look at this mess!" She said it quite loud because Uncle Court had just started the motor. She stepped across the cement platform and shouted at him, "Get the ladders! I want them all cleaned out right now!"

"Can't it wait till we get back?" Uncle Court turned the key off and put one foot out on the running board.

"No it can't wait. Those eggs are going to hatch any day. You need to get rid of them, right now!"

Uncle Court got out and motioned to Harold. As Harold lay his lacrosse stick down on the seat beside me, he said, "Shit!" but not loud enough for anyone else to hear. He jumped down and followed his father to the shed. We knew he was anxious to get to town. There was an open space beside the market where he and some other boys played lacrosse while their parents sat in the stalls with the stuff they had for sale.

When Harold and Uncle Court pushed their long ladders against the wall, the birds flew out and scattered in all directions, squawking loudly. Puggy and I slid down over the tailgate and stood by the platform to watch; Lester stayed in the cab. They reached into the nests and threw down handful after handful of eggs, which hit the cement and shattered into pieces of pale blue shell with yellow yolk oozing out. In a few minutes, they moved the ladders along to a new place and threw down more eggs. Then they were up again dropping more handfuls of eggs. One egg didn't break. It landed on an old rag mop left under the parlour window. Its shell was a light, greenish blue with tiny brown marks on it.

They went all around the house, moving the ladders a few feet at a time. Puggy and I followed them to the back. The poplar tree was full of noise because the starlings gathered there. When they were finished, Aunt Millie said, "Harold, clean up this mess. The rest of us better get to town before the market closes."

Harold was beside the bed of the truck with one hand on the side rail, ready to jump in. "Aw, no," he said. "I wanna go to town. I can clean it up when we get back."

"None of your lip, young man. Do as I say."

Harold reached in and grabbed his lacrosse stick. He threw it on the ground and kicked it. "Goddam you!" he said.

"Court, did you hear that? Now he's cursing!"

Uncle Court moved fast around the front of the truck and made a grab for him but Harold leapt away and disappeared through the kitchen door. Uncle Court stood still a moment, then he shouted after him, "You do as your mother says; get this all cleaned up by the time we get back! If you don't, you know what to expect. I'll give it to you good."

Before any of us had time to get into the truck, Harold appeared at the door again with a hammer in his hand. His little tabby cat was lapping at a smashed egg under the kitchen window. He scooped her up, set her down, and brought the hammer down on her head, once, twice, I don't know how many times. Her body flipped back and forth, her legs stiffened out, and then she was still. There was no sound. He let go of her and stood up straight, staring at Uncle Court, the hammer still in his hand.

Uncle Court motioned us all to get into the truck. He made the circle of the barnyard but came by the house again to call out the window. "Get that mess cleaned up. You hear?" He was almost past, so he stopped the truck long enough to yell, "And bury that goddam cat!"

TEN

FOR A LONG TIME AFTER SHE DIED, I TALKED TO MY MOTHER because some things I couldn't say to anyone else, like how hard it was to pass the room at the top of the stairs on my way to bed every night, and how I was afraid to go to the barn because sometimes Uncle Court would suddenly grab me and shove his hand between my legs. When I told her he did that to Annie before Aunt Ellen and Uncle Ben took her to live with them in Toronto and now he was doing it to me, my mother's voice was strong in my head. "Don't go to the barn."

But it was hard to stay away from the barn. The animals were there—the cats, and Dolly, and the Clydesdale team, the cows and calves—and the turnips. Aunt Millie didn't let us eat anything in the afternoon, even though we were very hungry after the long walk home from school. She'd say, "It will spoil your supper." We could have some milk. That suited Puggy okay but not me. After being with Aunt

Jane in Barrie and having pasteurized milk from the store, I couldn't drink the weak, blueish liquid that Aunt Millie kept in the pantry, all that was left after she separated the cream to make butter.

So I went to the barn for something to eat. I had a penknife of my own that I got at the Christmas church concert. I didn't like the boy who picked my name, but I liked the knife. It was silver. I kept it in the root cellar, hidden between two boards. There in the dark slant of the back wall of the barn, I reached into the bin to feel for a turnip. A small one was best because I could eat it all and not leave a trace. There were bins of potatoes and cabbages too but the turnips were best. I would slice off a little section of the peel and then scrape away until there was a juicy mound of flesh to suck, wet and sweet. Then another scrape, another suck. I kept the peels together and fed them to the calves on the way out.

Although I wasn't taking my mother's advice to stay out of the barn, in that dark corner I felt safe because Uncle Court never thought to look for me there. In that place I did most of my talking to my mother, but not always to tell her things; often, it was to remember, or try to remember, or to talk about how things were before she died. What she gave us to eat was the easiest, like the cottage cheese she made. When we were still in the Cariboo, in the wooden shack "on the crick," our milk went sour. She poured it from the pail into a cheesecloth and tied it on the clothesline. It hung there and dripped for a long time. When she took it down, she let us all have a little on a saucer, with salt and pepper. It was only one time, but that made it stronger in memory. After that, she kept the milk pail in the cold water of the creek.

We talked about when Annie and I started grade one together. We had lived in the small log schoolhouse the year before. When it went back to being a school, we felt good about the familiar smells of the old books and the pieces of chalk. It was far enough away from our ranch place that we had to take lunch. Some older cousins, who were living with us at the time, went to school with us. They were actually my mother's cousins; their father, Uncle Quinn, was her uncle, but a very young uncle because he was from her grandfather's second marriage. Their mother, Aunt Bessie, was Indian. Somebody said she and Uncle Quinn weren't married. My mother said that wasn't important and it wasn't anybody's business, even if they had five children: two girls, Laura and Delia, much older than us, Billy, between our ages who was starting grade one as well, a younger boy at home, and a brand new baby girl. We watched how Aunt Bessie (Great Aunt Bessie, really) opened the top of her dress and let a nipple come out for the baby to suck on. At noon, Laura and Delia brought the loaf of bread, the jar of peanut butter, and the long black-handled knife out of the gunny sack and set it on the teacher's desk. One would cut off slices, the other would spread on the peanut butter. It was bread our mother made. I told her I remembered the smell after school on the days she was baking, and how she let us put our own jam on while the slices were still warm. We were nine pupils altogether: five of us; two others starting school like Annie and me and Billy, one of whom was the son of the rancher our father worked for, the other an Indian girl who lived with her grandmother; and two sisters from the Jesmond

91

store. The two sisters brought their lunches in paper bags with sandwiches already made up. One day the younger one took out an orange, the first I had ever seen. She peeled it slowly, pulled off one section and put it in her mouth, then another, her eyes fastened on me with each bite, probably because I was staring so hard. The last section slipped from her fingers. She picked it up and looked it over. It had bits of grit on it from the board floor. She handed it to me. "Here, you can have it," she said. I took it eagerly, moved to the bucket by the wall, and swished it in the drinking water. The taste was sweet but at the same time a little bitter. The next time I saw oranges was on the train when we went East. The conductor came through the car with some, and I took one off his tray. My father and mother made me put it back because it cost money.

The only other food I could remember in the Cariboo was dried fruit—peaches and apricots, I think. You had to soak them in your mouth to make them soft enough to chew. No, there was one other thing. Duck for Christmas. But I didn't remember the actual dinner—only violent, jerky movements when our father brought home the live duck in a sack and set it down in the snow.

All these things I talked over with my mother by the turnip bin. Some I told her for the first time, others she knew about already. One that was hard to bring up was the cookie dancing on the hair in the kitchen at Rosewood Farm. There was a man guest sitting by the sideboard. My mother was stirring a pot at the stove. She told me I could have one of the cookies from the plateful on the table, so I took one and sat in a chair. With my first bite, a long hair broke free, its one end lodged firmly in the cookie. As I

92

chewed the smaller portion, I dangled the rest of the cookie on the end of the hair, making it skip and hop across the oilcloth toward the plate. The man smiled. As the cookie hit the plate with a clunk, my mother turned quickly from the stove with a horrified look. Trying to say I was sorry after she was dead didn't work: she said it was a terrible thing I did, making her so embarrassed in front of the young preacher.

Then there were things I couldn't talk to her about, things that had nothing to do with food. I would think them over there in the dark as I worked the thin blade into the flesh of a turnip.

There was my cousin Sheldon, the middle son of Uncle Harrington and Aunt Grace. Their farm was four miles up the concession from Rosewood. On their Saturday trips to town, and any other times they went by, they stopped on the way and on the way back, so we saw them a lot. There were three boys—Walter, Sheldon, and Ralph. Sheldon was three years older than me. The main things about him was that he smiled all the time, and that he liked me. He got me to sit beside him in the big rocking chair in the kitchen and he'd put his arm around me. I wasn't used to being hugged. It made me feel warm and safe. Mainly what we talked about was that the second one was always the best, and we'd go through all the family to prove it: he was certainly better than Walter, and I was way nicer than Annie; for all Lester was skinny and whiney like his mother, he was still not as mean as Harold; neither of us liked Mint, but we had to agree he wasn't as horrible as Angie. Sheldon even claimed it was true of the aunts and uncles too, that Aunt Jane in Barrie was the best of the

93

family. I didn't say anything because I secretly believed that Uncle Tee was the best, even though he wasn't the second oldest, but the third youngest.

One day Sheldon wanted me to go home with them. He said they were driving to town the next day again so it would be just overnight. I said I wouldn't be allowed. He said, "Sure you will. I know you want to. Let's go ask your mother."

We found her wringing out diapers in the back kitchen. Right away she said "No" and I turned to Sheldon and said, "See? I told you she wouldn't let me." A soppy diaper dropped back into the basin and her arm shot toward me. She gave me a hard slap on the face, which stung a lot because her hand was wet.

She never knew that that made me like Sheldon more than I did before. She never put her arms around me the way he did, nor the way she did when she sat with Puggy. My main picture of them together was Puggy standing between her knees with both our mother's arms around her. Even when I came back from Toronto with Aunt Ellen and Uncle Ben, she didn't hug me; she just said, "Hello, Virginnia." It sounded old and ordinary after they had been calling me "Ginnie" for the whole week. She didn't even call me "Bubba" anymore. But at least Sheldon came every week. We visited them sometimes on Sundays but I never did spend an overnight at their farm.

The talks I had with my mother and the thoughts I had to myself had been going on ever since she died, but the main ones, the important ones, were spread out over the winter during our second stay at Uncle Court's and Aunt Millie's, during the cold weather of Hawkestone when I was eating turnip in the gloom of the root cellar with the rank smell of the winter vegetables around me.

The episode I remembered closest to her death was the hardest to bring to mind and keep there. It was about pictures. There was a boxful of snapshots that my mother kept on her dresser in the room upstairs. It was a box that shoes from the catalogue came in. The label, addressed to our father, was still on it. I loved to look at the pictures. I was a fat baby in a fur-trimmed bonnet; a fat year-old wedged into a wash basin outside on the ground, one arm pushed down into a glass jar full of daisies; a chubby little girl in a ragged dress, holding a bowl. They were all me. And there were the three of us together: Annie and me with fair curly hair, holding onto Puggy's carriage; all of us outside with our father, him sitting on a straight wooden chair, a tall black cowboy hat on his head, Puggy in his lap, Annie squinting into the camera to his left, me standing sideways on the other side, my left hand resting on his right knee; one of our mother holding a horse, the three of us close together on its back. They were all pictures taken in the Cariboo, before we moved to Ontario.

It was a Saturday afternoon near the middle of October. I came down the stairs with the box in my arms. Our mother was sweeping near the bottom of the stairway. Somehow I lost my grip, the box fell, and the lid flew off, scattering pictures all the way to the bottom. In an instant, I was on my knees, scooping them into the box, backing down step by step.

She looked over her shoulder, the broom upright in her hands. She leaned wearily on it. "You are a very clumsy girl," she said. "When I'm dead you'll remember you made this awful mess. Then, what will you think?"

I picked up every picture, put the lid on the box, and took it back upstairs.

Once I had actually made her say the words again, there in the root cellar, I carefully gathered up all the peelings and the last of the turnip and walked out along the passageway. The calves looked up expectantly, then ducked their heads to the floor when I dropped the handful. Outside in the cold air, I turned toward the house, ugly even in the snow, my hand tightly gripping the closed knife in the pocket of my coat.

ELEVEN

WE DIDN'T KNOW ABOUT AUNT HELENA AT ALL UNTIL SHE AND
Uncle Tee got married one spring. I was nine and a half
and in grade five; we were back at Hawkestone with Uncle
Court and Aunt Millie for the second time. But that fall
they sent us to Aunt Jane's and Uncle Elliott's again in
Barrie, where I started grade six. No matter which of the
places we lived at, we got to visit Rosewood Farm nearly
every week. We first met Aunt Helena there because she
and Uncle Tee took over the upstairs for their own living
quarters, I think because Uncle Tee knew better than to
have his wife live with Grandma. They fixed up the big
room at the top of the back stairs, which used to be the
hired man's, as a kitchen. They put in a sink and pump, in
the corner right over the sink and pump in the big kitchen
below.

But that was the only way the two kitchens were at
all alike. Grandma used a kind of whitewash (she called it

calcimine) on the walls and ceiling. Everything else—the doorways and the window frames, the high wainscoting that went completely around the room, the cabinets and sideboard, and the table and chairs—Grandma had painted what Aunt Helena called "apple green." Aunt Helena explained to Puggy and me that she liked to have a colour scheme, and she had chosen buff and red. Buff was a colour we had never heard of. So the cabinets and table and chairs were a pale brown colour, like a tan. It didn't look very good by itself but with the red trim it was prettier than anything we'd ever seen. The walls were papered instead of whitewashed. The background was buff and the pattern was of little brown houses with green trees around them. All the houses had red roofs and all the trees had red apples. As soon as I saw Aunt Helena, and her kitchen, I knew she was the one I wanted to live with. Aunt Jane was really nice but we couldn't have her without getting Angie and Mint too. As for Aunt Millie, her whiny voice was enough, never mind the strappings and the ugly house. I already felt closer to Uncle Tee than to Uncle Elliott, or even our father, and Uncle Court I tried to keep out of my mind. The last time at their place I had to keep watch, to remember where he was, to make sure never to be alone with him in the barn or down by the creek.

After Uncle Tee got married and we went to visit our grandparents, the first thing I did every time was call up the stairs to Aunt Helena. She'd say, "Is that you Bubba?" and tell me to come right up. She called me Bubba because Uncle Tee did. They both said it suited me better than Virginnia, or even Ginnie. I liked that because no one else ever talked about whether anything suited me or not. And she talked to me as though I was important, not just a kid who didn't know much. She even asked me for advice. She said she knew quite a bit about dogs because she had a big Scotch collie called Mac at home in Toronto with her parents, but she didn't know anything about cats. How did they like to be petted, did they like to have their ears scratched the way dogs did? I had never thought much about it before but I helped her as much as I could, explaining that they didn't like hard scratching so much as soft petting and long strokes, and I showed her how the barn cat Fluffy raised up when you slid your hand along her back to the base of her tail. Aunt Helena tried it. She said, "Oh, I see what you mean!" No one had ever said that to me before. The next time I went up the stairs to visit, she had two little kittens. One was a tortoise-shell, the other was white with a few black patches. She called them Sally and Irma. That was the first time I'd heard of proper names for cats. They were girls' names really. That was something else different about Aunt Helena.

Sometimes when we were there she would take me on a walk. She would get dressed especially for it. She wore what she called breeks. They were a brown woolly material with tight legs that pouched out sideways at the knees. She said she made them herself. She had a short jacket, dark brown, a light brown (maybe buff) slouchy cap, high black boots, and bright red lipstick. And she climbed over fences. I couldn't think of her as an aunt at all. All my other aunts wore clothes like my grandmother's: print house dresses and plain low shoes. If they ever went walking, they stayed on the road and used gates.

So I knew she was the one I wanted to live with. I made

myself as nice as I could whenever I was with her. I wanted her to like me so much that she would ask me to come and stay. But I couldn't think of many ways to get that to happen. I asked her a lot of questions about her kittens and her clothes, and her dog Mac that she had to leave with her parents in the city. She asked me questions too, mostly about school, and it was good to have someone to tell about my bird-sighting project (I had only five starlings and a blue jay and eleven sparrows so far but I'd soon have a lot more when the robins and bluebirds came back), and about the play our class was putting on with Marie Graham as Snow White because she was the jeweler's daughter, and she got to sing "Some Day My Prince Will Come," and David Saunders was the prince, and I got to help with twining the paper flowers and leaves around the wishing well. She even asked me if I liked to read. No one had ever done that before.

She stayed real interested all the way along the lane to the maple bush at the back of the farm while I told her the story of a book I got from the library, *The Secret Garden*. When I finished the part about the garden being a success and the boy cousin getting cured, she asked me if I liked planting things. I said I did but I had to tell her the only time I ever tried it was when we were at Hawkestone and we got to pick a package of seeds at school for a growing project and I picked snapdragons because I liked the name. I planted them where Aunt Millie said I could, in a raised bed behind the house, but they never came up . The earth was too hard at that place. Even when it rained. I was very disappointed. The flowers on the side of the package looked real pretty.

Well, I don't know whether it was because I wished so hard, or because I tried so hard, but it actually did happen that Aunt Helena wanted me—and it was because of Angie. During the fall and winter months in Barrie, she seemed to be getting more and more mean about us living with them and she kept complaining to her mother, saying Aunt Jane liked us better than her and that there wasn't enough room for us all in that little house and that we should be sent out West to our father. Aunt Jane couldn't do anything but plead with her to be nice.

It was noon. We were home for lunch. Puggy and I sat at the kitchen table with peanut butter sandwiches and milk. Angie wasn't usually home at that time of day because she did housework for several families and was away all day except for the few times she finished early. She stood in the doorway with a banana in her hand. The peeled back parts flopped from side to side as she waved it about. "I can't stand them here any longer. Look how crowded it is. There's no room for me even to sit down."

Aunt Jane turned from the sideboard where she was punching down bread dough. "We didn't know you were going to be home today, did we? Come on, girls, pull the table out."

We stood up, but before we even got our chairs out of the way, Angie said, "Oh, don't bother. I hate eating with you anyway. I'm going to write a letter to your dad, right now, and tell him he has to take you."

Aunt Jane grabbed up the bottom of her apron and wiped flour from her hands. "Now, that isn't nice. You know our Lord can hear you. He wants you to be a good Christian girl and maybe He's testing you to see how you treat your cousins. They're orphans, remember."

"Then they should be in an orphanage!" Angie freed
what was left of the banana and threw the peel on the table.
"And if God is testing me, then I'm never going to His old
mission again until they're gone. That'll be a test for Him!"
As her bedroom door slammed, Aunt Jane pushed us gently
back onto our chairs. Her hand left a floury imprint on the
sleeve of Puggy's navy blue sweater.

No one wrote to our father. No one sent us to an
orphanage. Instead, Aunt Jane said we would go back to
Uncle Court's. They had a big house, she said, and it would
be better for us to be in the country anyway. Since Aunt
Jane and Uncle Elliott didn't have a car, we would have to
wait until someone came down for a visit, Uncle Court or
Uncle Tee maybe. But something had to be done sooner,
because Aunt Jane and Uncle Elliott were afraid Angelica
would stop going to church. So that was how we came to
be with Angie on Saturday, hitch-hiking on the highway
from Barrie to Hawkestone.

We started early in the morning. There wasn't much
traffic. Apart from when a car was approaching and we
stood in a line, all three, with our thumbs out, we just
kept walking. At least Puggy and I didn't have to carry
anything. Angie had clean bloomers and stockings for both
of us in her big red purse. Aunt Jane would send our things
later. Walking, walking. The pavement hot through our
thin soles. The gravel at the edge bumpy and sometimes
sharp.

Angie said we should go slow and look very tired so
the drivers would feel sorry for us. I thought Puggy had a
better idea when she said we should walk fast so it looked

as though we were in a hurry, as though it was important to get somewhere quick. We tried both ways but no car stopped.

The two towns we knew: Barrie and Orillia, thirty miles apart. And the three farms we knew: Uncle Court's at Hawkestone, halfway between, with Aunt Mae's nearby; and Rosewood, four miles the other side of Orillia, to the north.

Finally we turned off on the side road that led to Uncle Court's and Aunt Millie's. Only a mile and three-quarters more to go, Angie said. Not long after, a cloud of dust appeared at a far bend in the road and, just ahead of it, we could make out Uncle Court's old Ford truck. When it stopped beside us, Uncle Court said, "Get in back. That's an extra expense for your Aunt Jane, having to phone to get me to meet you." Angie was already climbing onto the front seat beside him. He leaned over to kiss her and she put her lips right up against his.

The forgotten look of bare wood floors and smoke-dark walls, the forgotten smell of sour towels and soaking rags—all suddenly familiar again. And Aunt Millie bending to kiss us. Had that ever happened before? Puggy first, then me. The surprise to feel the wrinkles of her cheek, which always looked as though creased in rock, press in softly against my mouth.

When she straightened up again, she said, "Your Uncle Tee just phoned. They'll be over later, maybe stay for supper." She reached her hand to Puggy's shoulder, then turned to me. "Well, Virginnia, your Aunt Helena wants to take you." Those were the words—the long-awaited words. All the bluebirds were loosed and flying around me, my

103

snapdragons were up and blooming bright yellow, roses from *The Secret Garden* were overflowing onto the bare boards of the kitchen floor. I knew better than to move. Stand stock still. Stare straight ahead. Don't let anyone know....

Aunt Millie pulled Puggy in close to her. "And Sylvie, you're going to be my little girl. Maybe you can take guitar lessons like Harold. Would you like that?" Puggy's cheek was pushed crooked against the faded print of Aunt Millie's apron. Her eyes were shut, her lips tight together. By the water bucket behind them, Uncle Court, raising the tin dipper to his lips, looked sideways at us.

It was a long time before they came. They couldn't stay for supper. It wasn't just that they had to get back to milk the cows and do the chores. Two of their ewes were late with their lambs, so they didn't want to be away long. Uncle Tee and Uncle Court sat together on the small couch under the window and smoked. Lester crawled up on Uncle Tee's knee and started grabbing his nose between his forefinger and his thumb. Uncle Tee held his cigarette aside and tickled him with the other hand. There were other sounds—Angie setting out cups and saucers, Aunt Millie poking at the fire in the stove to get the kettle boiling, and the bounce, bounce of Harold's lacrosse ball on the cement outside.

Aunt Helena sat down in a chair by the table. She wore her navy blue silk dress, the one she got married in. The string of pearls too. She leaned over toward Puggy and me, squeezed together in the wooden rocking chair. She said, "Bubba, would you like to come and live with me?"

I didn't move, or nod, or anything. Did I even breathe?

I looked straight into her eyes. I think that was the first time I realized they were green, with dark flecks in them, just like mine.

"Yes, I would. But," I added, real fast so it would be sure to come out, "not unless Puggy can come too."

TWELVE

I LIKED LYING BACK IN THE MANGER, PULLING THE HAY OUT FROM under me and piling it on my stomach, with Tony's head above me, temples pulsing in and out as he chewed. The manger was high on each side but I could see Bert in the next stall and, through the spaces between the boards, some of the cows. They were straining against their stanchions, reaching out their necks with heads sideways, working the cement of the feed-alley with their tongues for stray bits of chaff. I pulled the oat tin out from under the hay and scooped up a handful. His lips, hanging loose, moved together on my hand, replacing oats with green saliva. I rubbed it off on the timothy heads and reached back into the pail.

The familiar ache was there, at the spot just under the bone in the middle of my chest. When we came back to Rosewood to stay and I saw Tony almost full-grown standing in the stall next to his mother, it lodged there, as though it was my very centre, like the maypole at school with streamers coming out of it. But not streamers. More like fine rope or spider lines, floating up to Tony and around him and down again to that spot, the bottom of the inverted maypole. It was over his head like a canopy. Over his long, dark ears, his forelock, and his moving temples. Maybe like a parachute, its silken chords coming down to me, crowding into the one spot, pinned together in me. It was an inside hurt, not a hurt like a headache—not like the headaches I used to have—and it came only when I was with him.

I liked to pull his head down and hold the leather of his halter so I could feel him chewing against my cheek, through my head, and down to my chest. I hugged his head, until he stopped chewing, and I could hear both our heartbeats.

I remember one particular Saturday, with every detail, because it was the first day I wrote down things that happened. Aunt Helena said it would be a good idea and she bought me a special scribbler, not the kind with the rough paper for pencil writing but the kind with dark lines and smooth paper for ink. I had finished reading all the books we picked out at the library in town. She said if I was going to read that fast, I might as well write a lot too, and that way I could "justify the teacher's expectations" after she had put me ahead a grade the year before.

When I wrote things down—what happened and how I felt about them—I remembered everything much better. That is why the day that began with me in Tony's manger is so vivid. The cows had been fed already and were stretching to get the last of the hay from the cement in front of them. Uncle Tee and Murray were milking. Murray lived down near the highway, across from Old Ed's place. He didn't stay at Rosewood but came up every day in busy seasons to help out, except on Sundays. And he had Saturday afternoons off too. He wasn't just an ordinary hired man; he got paid and everything, but he was Uncle Tee's best friend.

Uncle Tee set his pail of milk on the wide sill of the stable window and began to roll a cigarette, pushing the milk stool along the cement floor with his boot until he was directly behind one of the red and white cows, the one called Willis. Grandad had named her after the farmer he bought her from, John Willis over on the Town Line. Uncle Tee sat on the stool, his back against the wall, slowly rolled tobacco into shape between his thumbs and forefingers, gave a long lick with his tongue, then poked the straggly ends of tobacco in with a match. "Here you are, Murr." Uncle Tee was the only one who called him Murr. He twisted the paper at one end and handed the cigarette over. Murray took it, accepted a light, then went back to milking, his red hair leaning into Willis' red flank. Through the cracks in the manger, I could imagine that the smoke rising on each side of him was the frothy sound from the fresh milk escaping the pail between his knees.

Uncle Tee rolled another cigarette, this time for himself. "You nearly finished her?"

"Just startin' on the back. You didn't want me to strip her right out this mornin' did you?"

"No. We'd better get her dried up. Should be dropping her calf any time now. You can cut her down to one milking a day by the first of the week. I sure hope she doesn't give us any trouble this time. She's looking pretty big."

The stanchions clicked and rattled with the movements of the cows. One of the calves in the far pen started to bawl, heaving out then jerking in again for the next bellow. "Those calves are hungry. Guess I'd better start separating so Bubba can get some milk to them. Where is she anyway?"

"She was over givin' the horses their oats. Probably in with Tony. You know how she is about that horse." Murray got up from beside Willis, the pail in one hand. He picked up the stool. "Why don't you let me do the separatin' this mornin'? Didn't you want to have a look at the bins up in the granary and figure out what to use for seed?"

"Okay. Good idea. It looks like a fair day. I could start the bottom field this morning." Uncle Tee took his jacket from a nail near the door and went around the row of cows to the feed alley. As he passed Tony's manger, he said, "Out of there now, Bub. Go give Murr a hand." He put on his jacket as he headed for the ladder to the loft.

I stood up and brushed the bits of hay off my shirt and pants. I pressed my mouth against the flat part of Tony's nose between the two nostrils and felt his warmth, and breathed his smell. Something pungent in it gave me a sense of excitement. I ran my fingers through his forelock and eased strands of hair out from under the headband. I climbed out into the feed passage and emptied what was left in the bucket into his oat box. His head swung over to it. The other horses had finished theirs, Bert on one side, standing with his ears laid back and his mouth hung loose, Bette, on the other, rummaging in her hay.

In the milk room Murray turned the handle of the

separator. I liked to see the cream came out the short spout at the side and drop into the small container on the high stand that was attached to the machine, and the skim milk come out the long spout at the front and drop into the large pail on the floor. Uncle Tee had explained how the separation of milk and cream worked, but I still didn't really understand it. As I poured the skim milk into feed buckets, I asked Murray when he thought Willis would have her calf, but he only shouted, "Eh? What'd you say, kid? You know I can't hear you over this damned machine. You'd better get those calves fed!"

When I lowered the buckets over the side of the pen, the two calves plunged their noses into the froth and came up snorting and spluttering. Looking at their stiff bodies, tails held high, legs angling out with hooves placed solidly in the straw of the floor, I remembered how Tony looked when he was a foal. He was completely black and his mane shagged out in all directions; he stepped around high on his long legs as if he knew all about what he was and was real proud of it. Even now that he was grown up, he was like that. But not Bert. Bert kept his head hung down, and was mean. A few months before, he bit me hard on the hand when I tried to catch him in the barnyard. Uncle Tee took the pitchfork to him when he found out. It was as though Bert had forgotten what it was like to be young. Tony was one of the kind that would never forget. He would always seem young.

The calves finished the milk but kept bunting the empty pails and sucking at the bit left in the bottom. I had to pull up hard on the handles then drop the pails down fast, to get them free from their heads. Then the black calf went straight for the red one's ear, closing his foamy mouth over it. As he sucked on it, his legs were set like four props and his body jerked with the bunting movement. The red calf simply stood. I wondered which of them would remember, and which forget.

I went back along the feed alley to the milk room. As I passed Tony, I caught his halter and pressed my head against his chewing again. He snorted and pulled away.

When I got in to breakfast it was still only about five-thirty, but Puggy was already at the kitchen door shaking out the mop. Grandma didn't let her go out to the barn with me; she said there were plenty of chores for her to do in the house. Puggy gave the mop a little shake, pointed it in the direction of our grandparents' bedroom, then went inside. I walked up the back stairs to the bright red and buff kitchen which smelled of bacon and eggs. Aunt Helena poured my coffee. From the time I came to live with them they let me drink coffee, if two thirds of the cup was milk.

That was how that Saturday began.

About three in the afternoon, Aunt Helena made up a pail of lemonade and asked me to take it to Uncle Tee, who was on the seeder in the lower field. It was in a tin honey pail that had a picture of a beehive on the side with bees flying both ways. We got our honey from Barney Stoker, about a mile up the Seventh Concession—so much clover honey every year, and so much buckwheat. There were always lots of empty pails by spring. I liked to read what was printed on the side:

> All pure honey will granulate. To
> liquify, place container in warm

water no hotter than the hand can
bear and allow to stand until the
honey becomes perfectly clear.

It sounded like a poem to me. If you read it right, it
even rhymed, kind of:

All pure honey
will granulate.
To liquify
place container in warm water
no hotter
than the hand can bear
and allow to stand
until the honey becomes
perfectly clear.

I said it over and over in my head until I came to the
stone fence that separated the top field from the bottom
one. I set the pail on a flat stone on top and crawled up. I
could see Uncle Tee on the seed-drill behind the team on
the far side of the field. The rocks were uneven but the
fence was wide enough for me to walk along the top. If I
went to the corner and waited, he could have a drink of
lemonade in the shade when he came around that way.

The day was itself, and all around me, a day to
remember because it was different from every other day,
just as yesterday was different from the day before that, and
tomorrow would be different from today. All the different
days piled up, one on top of the other, like all the rocks
there under me, and pretty soon there was something solid,

like the wide stone wall, that was called the past. Today was always on the top, tomorrow was something waiting somewhere to settle into being today on top of yesterday, and the fence got higher and higher. Uncle Tee's was pretty high. "I remember when we were kids and they were putting the highway through." How far down did he have to reach to find that stone? And why was it that you could take one moment out of the middle, or even the bottom, and not loosen the whole structure or change its shape?

At the corner where the rock fence met the fence-row of basswood, I jumped down and set the pail in the shade. I sat beside it and looked at the trees of the fence-row and thought how they reached into the sky and how the clouds came down to look through their branches. What would it feel like to be a tree? to really be thinking and feeling from inside the bark and to know all the roots were part of you, and all the branches? And what about when the leaves started to come out? You probably wouldn't feel that any more than when your hair grows, or your fingernails. But where would your eyes be? From inside myself looking out, as much as I tried to centre things somewhere else, it was always right behind my eyes that was "me." "I" am right here, in this spot. Everything else—arms, legs, stomach, ears—are just "parts " of me. I remembered how the maple in the pasture looked last summer when it was all leaves, and how I felt myself huge as though I could put my arms around it. Where were its eyes?

Uncle Tee was turning the team at the far end of the field. Even from where I sat on the ground I could see that Bert was hanging back in the traces, letting Bette do all the work. Bette just kept on going, doing more than her

113

share. Maybe when Tony was old enough to take over for her Bert would do more pulling. But not likely. Uncle Tee said he was born lazy. I thought about the oats. Bert and Bette planting oats, so they could eat more oats, to keep in good shape so they could plant more oats, to eat. And at every step they took, hundreds of seeds fell to the ground to sprout and grow. If they got stopped halfway down, or even nine-tenths of the way down, it would all be different. The seeds have to get to the earth and then they will sprout and grow up in rows, in the exact pattern forming at this very minute. I stood up. It was as though I had scooped a moment out of time and held it in my hand like a stone and looked at it and thought about how I would always remember it and then, instead of adding it to the wall, I let it go flying away from me, out over the rock wall and across the pasture to the west, to where there was a tree standing alone.

It was an old birch tree. Even when all the branches were bare, you could still tell which parts were already dead. How could anything be partly dead? Maybe like Old Ed's arm that hung straight and loose at his side, but that was paralyzed, not really dead; it still had blood in it and everything. It was a red birch. The bark was the same kind that any birch tree had, except it was a reddish-brown colour. Uncle Tee had explained the difference to me. It was too far away to see the horizontal markings in the bark but it was about the colour of Murray's hair, or the colour of that rock beside it. I didn't remember a big rock like that, not there!

I got to the top of the fence where I could see better. It was a cow, and not just lying normally under the tree, but

114

on its side. The rock shape was the mound of the belly. It was Willis! I was down off the fence and running toward the seed-drill. Shouting: "Uncle Tee! Uncle Tee! It's Willis! She's having her calf!" He stopped the team and cupped his hand to his ear. I yelled again. He threw the reins up over Bette's back and dropped the ends to the ground. We ran together across the upper field but by the time I got to the pasture he was way ahead of me. Even before I got to the birch I could see Willis' head stretched out on the grass, her eyes bulging.

Uncle Tee was on his knees beside her; he snatched up her tail and looked under it, then slid his hand along her belly. "Oh Christ! It's not the calf! She's bloated." He jumped to his feet. "I'll have to cut...." He was working his hand into one pocket, then another. "God Almighty! Where's my goddam knife!" His hands at his side turned outward in an empty gesture. "Goddam it! It's in my other pants. She's got to be punctured right away or she won't make it."

I reached into my back pocket and held out my penknife. "Will this work?"

The sliver of silver looked so small and insignificant that I was sure the offer was useless, but he grabbed it and flicked out the blade. "Good girl!" And he was down beside her again. I saw his quick jab, heard the explosion of air, smelled the immediate stench as it swooshed past me and out into the pasture. It smelled like rotting turnips, and I dizzied back into my time of root cellar and decaying vegetables, losing track of what else Uncle Tee was doing and of how much time was passing. Then he said, "That does it! She'll be fine." He wiped the blade on his pant leg,

115

closed the knife and handed it back to me. Willis raised her head and struggled to her feet.

I stayed with her while Uncle Tee went back to the field to unhook the team and drive them to the stable. He said he wouldn't take time to unharness them, just put them in their stalls. By the time he came back, Willis was starting slowly along the roadway toward the barn. Uncle Tee and I walked one on each side of her. He looked across at me, his hand on her back. "We did it Bubba. We saved her."

But that Saturday wasn't over yet. When it was more than half an hour past suppertime and Uncle Tee hadn't come in yet, Aunt Helena asked me to go look for him. She had put the meat and vegetables in the oven to keep them warm and she didn't want them to dry out.

I knew he hadn't taken the team back out to the field so I went straight to the barn. The horses were eating hay, their harnesses off, and, as I moved along the pens, I saw Willis in one of them. Fresh straw was deep all around her and, standing on long wobbly legs, its head making bobbing motions at her udder, was a small calf. Its hide was a reddish colour. The familiar ache of the morning jolted into my chest. I wanted to jump into the pen and be with the little thing and maybe get it to pull its head back so I could see if it had a white patch on its face like its mother, but it was shiny wet all over and, anyway, I had to find Uncle Tee. He had been right when he said it could be anytime now.

I went past the row of empty stanchions and out the cowbarn door. I could hear noises coming from the other side of the gangway, which sloped up to the top floor where the hay mows and the granary were.

Uncle Tee was behind the root cellar, out in the sheep pasture, working a shovel into a heap of dirt. "So Willis had her calf already!" I shouted as I crossed the gangway. He was scooping up the earth and throwing it into a shallow depression, then stomping it flat with his boots.

He looked over at me, one hand on the upright shovel, still moving his feet up and down. "Yes, she had it all right. Probably getting bloated like that brought it on sooner. But she had twins. Both little heifers." He gave a final stomp, then struck the ground hard with the shovel. "One didn't make it."

On the way to the house, after putting the shovel back in its place in the driving shed, he rested one hand on my shoulder. "Bubba, I think it would be a good idea if we don't tell your Aunt Helena the whole story. We can just say one was born. Okay?" I nodded my head and felt his fingers tighten. We were both thinking the same thing.

It is hard to express what we were both remembering because it happened a few months back, before I started to write down all these things. Aunt Helena was going to have a baby. She had a name already, Barbara Carol, because she was sure it was going to be a girl. I felt good when she said she really liked girls better; she thought little boys smelled funny. She and Uncle Tee were very happy.

But what would have been that little baby girl was buried in the flower garden on the north side of the house. Aunt Helena was still sick in bed and a big bucket sat at the top of the back stairs. A cat fight started up there while I was out getting an armful of wood. I heard a loud crash and a series of bumping noises and then two tomcats streaked past me. When I got to the bottom of the stairs and saw

117

what they had done, I dropped the wood and ran to the shed to get Uncle Tee. He was hammering the last nails into a little plywood box he had just made. We went down to the house together. He didn't want me to help him but I did. We scraped everything off the stairs, step by step.

THIRTEEN

WHEN I TOLD AUNT HELENA I WOULDN'T GO WITH HER AND UNCLE Tee unless Puggy could come with me, it turned out different than I expected. They did take us both to Rosewood, but Puggy had to live downstairs with Grandma and Grandad. Because of the expense, they said. I guess they had all talked it over beforehand. I was worried that Puggy would feel hurt but she said at least it would be better than being with Uncle Court and Aunt Millie, and Harold and Lester. "And I'm glad to have Grandad," she said.

Right away it was different for me. Mostly because I got to have things of my own. For instance, the first time they went to town after I got there, Aunt Helena bought me a toothbrush, a blue one with a white handle. She showed me how to squeeze paste out of the tube onto the bristles, and she told me the proper way to brush was up and down, not sideways. When I was finished, she got the hammer and drove a nail into the side of the cabinet so I could hang my toothbrush beside hers and Uncle Tee's.

Another thing was a bedroom of my own. It was the big room on the north side of the house. There were two full-sized beds in it, one against each wall, with lots of space between them. She said Puggy was to come upstairs to sleep in my room because Grandma was using the second bedroom downstairs for her toilet. Grandad and Uncle Tee had built a platform in there and set up a commode for her after she slipped when she was lowering herself down onto the chamber pot. I guess because she was so fat, she somehow hit it sideways, cracking the porcelain and spilling everything that was already in it out on the floor. Someone still had to empty the pail from under the seat of the commode, but the whole thing was a lot easier and safer.

Maybe the best thing of all, though, was a kitten. Aunt Helena said I was to have one of Sally's new litter. But I couldn't decide on a name for it. I had always thought that if I had a cat of my own I would call her Nancy but now that I had chosen the only one of the five that was all black, the name didn't seem right. Aunt Helena suggested that I get everyone, including the kids at school, to think of a good name and write it down. Then I could look over them and see if there was one I liked. So that was what I did. I set all the slips of paper out on the kitchen table as soon as I got home. About ten of them said "Blackie," a few said "Darkie," some "Fluffy," one was "Midnight," and four had girls' names: "Molly," "Daisy," "Fifi," and "Topsy." The only one I really liked was "Topsy" which I knew was Aunt Helena's because of her handwriting and also because she had already told me about a book called *Uncle Tom's Cabin* which had a little black girl named "Topsy" in it. So, at last I had a kitten all my own, and I called her "Topsy."

I also had more clothes than I was ever used to. Aunt Helena made me a new dress. It was brown cotton and it came way above my knees. It let the air come up cool underneath. As soon as Uncle Tee saw me wearing it, he started calling me "Brownie," and that was his name for me all summer. I didn't have to wear long stockings any more; I wore ankle socks, or no socks at all if I felt like it. They even let me wear shorts and slacks, ones that Aunt Helena's niece had grown out of. Grandma thought it was wrong to let me go around that way, and one day she stopped me at the foot of the back stairs. "Come here!" she said. She pulled at my shorts to try to make them longer. "It's sinful in the Lord's eyes for a girl to show bare flesh like this!" When the hem of my shorts was down to my knees and my bare stomach popped out beneath my blouse, she said, "You get upstairs and put on something decent! You'll have boys pinching your bottom! I don't want you teaching your sister such sinful ways."

Puggy and I weren't together very much except for bedtime and the hour in the mornings and afternoons walking to and from school. We had a bed each. The bedsteads were shiny brass and the quilts were heaped high because the mattresses underneath were stuffed full of straw. I liked to wriggle my body down into the rustling fullness, and gradually, over the first week, I made a hollow for myself that stretched diagonally across the bed. I am sure I did not move from it the whole night through. As I was ready to drop off, I tried to think back to what it was like before I came to Rosewood. But there was never time. How could

121

I be awake at night one moment, and the next moment it would be morning?

In the corner of the room by the window was a brown dresser. The top two drawers were for me and the bottom two for Puggy. We each had a wooden orange crate, stood on end so it had one shelf, beside our beds, and there were nails on the back of the door to hang up clothes. Uncle Tee brought in two small rugs for us which he had tanned and finished himself from the hides of lambs that had died in the winter. "To step on when you get out of bed on cold mornings," he said.

But it wasn't cold yet. The days, and the nights too, kept getting warmer. We had a screen to let in fresh air and to keep out the mosquitoes but it didn't seem to work very well. You had to push up the window and hold it there while you put the screen in place on the sill, then close the window down on it. I had to get Puggy to help me. There was a sliding part, but even with it extended against the frame, mosquitoes got in. There was a fat, brown, hard-shelled beetle that got in too, even though there wasn't possibly enough space for an insect that huge. I really believed that it hatched out in the room because it mostly hung on the wallpaper near the window making a scritching sound with its legs as though it wanted to get out. Every once in a while it would zoom across the room, hit against the wall, and drop to the floor. When I told Uncle Tee, he said it was harmless; it was just a June bug. Mostly I didn't mind things like spiders or toads or snakes; in fact, Puggy and I made ourselves pick up every snake we could get hold of when we happened to see one out in the bush or along the road. That way, we didn't have to run

122

off screaming like all the other girls when the boys chased us and tried to put one down our neck. But the June bugs were a different matter. Even though I loved the room, I could hardly bear to go into it for fear one would zip across and hit me.

Often, at bed-time, I hurried in, slid under the covers with all my clothes on, and waited for Puggy to come upstairs. Then I'd whisper loudly, "June Bug!" Without saying a word she would drag the chair over by the window, get onto it and then onto the dresser. From there she could pick off the June bug in her hankie. Once I was sure it was caught, I would get up and push open the screen far enough for her to put it out. When I asked her why those fat hard beetles didn't bother her she said that since her birthday was in June she was sure they were friendly to her.

There were other reasons our bed-time was special. The days were getting longer but we still had to light a lamp to go to bed by, and one night, as I was about to blow it out, Aunt Helena came into our room with a book under her arm. She said, "I think you two need tucking in." She poked the quilts in around me and pushed a bit at the pillow. Then she went over to Puggy's bed and did the same. I was getting ready to do my burrowing down into the straw when she pushed the chair over near the lamp on my crate. "How would you like me to read to you a little before you go to sleep?" Puggy and I both sat up. We had never heard of such a thing. It's true that I used to read to Puggy, but that was when she was only in grade one and two and couldn't read very well herself, but no one had ever read to us! She showed us the book; it was called *Black Beauty* and had the picture of a horse's head on the cover. Aunt Helena said the title of Chapter One

123

was "My Early Home." When she started reading I knew I would never forget the way it began: "The first place that I can well remember, was a large, pleasant meadow with a pond of clear water in it." Even though she had told us it was a horse talking, the place he described was just like the very first place I could remember too, the little ranch our mother and father had in the Cariboo. Even before the beginning of the next sentence, Puggy jumped out of her bed and scrambled up onto mine. Without lifting her eyes from the book, Aunt Helena pulled back my covers so Puggy could get in with me. We both lay back and listened,watching her lips. How could she read while she was smiling so much?

Going to and from school was the only other time Puggy and I had together. Since it was May when we went to Rosewood, most of the wild flowers were up. On the shortcut, we had to cross several bush lots, open fields, and pastures, so we were able to find all the different kinds. Every afternoon we came home with a new bouquet. We didn't know the names of many of them but Aunt Helena told us some, and if she didn't know, Uncle Tee did for sure. There were violets, some deep blue or purple, some yellow, and another flower that looked like a violet except it was white with dark markings that they said was a johnny-jump-up. The mayflowers were white with round petals, the adder tongues yellow with dark spots, and the trillium had only three petals, and could be either dark red or pure white. At school all the kids knew that the trillium, the white one, was the special flower of Ontario and that was why you weren't supposed to pick it. They asked us what British Columbia's special flower was but we didn't know.

When the teacher heard us talking about it, she gave us a reference book all about Canada, and we looked it up. It said it was dogwood, but we had never heard of it before.

My favourite of all was jack-in-the-pulpit. He stood up straight just as though he was an extension of the long stem, and the flower part was only one petal that wrapped around itself like a tall striped cloak with a pointed top that tipped down so it looked like a hood. Inside was a long, thin, yellow shaft. Uncle Tee said that was Jack himself, but that it was really the flower's pistil.

Once in a while we gave some of the flowers to our grandmother. She always smiled when she took them but if there was a jack-in-the-pulpit among them, she would pull it out of the bouquet and throw it away. She said it was sinful to think of such an ugly flower as a preacher of God's word.

To me, it wasn't an ugly flower at all; in fact, it was because of it that I got started on a whole new project. One day when Puggy and I were on our way home from school, I bent down to pick what I thought would be the last jack-in-the-pulpit of my bouquet, because we were nearing the edge of the maple bush alongside Old Mr. Carson's sugar shack with his open barnyard ahead of us. For some reason, with that particular flower, the stem didn't snap off as they usually did and the whole thing came up out of the ground. I could have broken off the stem and poked the rest back into the hole it had come out of but the sight of the white bulb with bits of earth clinging to the small roots at the bottom gave me the idea that I could plant it somewhere at home. I could start a garden of my own—a secret garden, with maybe nothing in it but wild flowers.

I wrapped the bulb carefully in my hankie and stuffed it into the pocket of my dress, holding myself straight so I wouldn't break off the flower part that was sticking up. Then I waited for Puggy to catch up. I didn't tell her what I had decided to do. It was such a wonderful secret.All the rest of the way home—across Carsons' yard and out their lane, down the main road to our lane, and then up to the house—I tried to imagine where my garden would be. Grandma was waiting at the downstairs kitchen door with a rag mop in her hands. There was a bucket of water, with a bar of yellow soap floating in it, on the stone step beside her. "There you are finally," she said. "How can you be so long getting home from school? You shouldn't waste time picking flowers." She took Puggy's bouquet from her and pushed the mop into her hands. "Here, give the verandah a good scrubbing. The starlings have been roosting in there and messing up the floor." She went back into the house without having even looked at me. Puggy dropped her school bag on the step, picked up the pail, and moved along the wall toward the front of the house. Her body was bent to the side under the weight; one of her long brown stockings sagged down so far it covered the back part of her shoe.

I had chores to do, too, but mostly they were just for after supper: throwing hay down from the loft for the horses and cattle in the main barn, putting alfalfa in the mangers for the sheep in the adjoining building, and scattering grain for the hens outside. My only job after school was gathering eggs. There were usually two or three in each nest box, so as long as I took out a big enough basket I didn't have to make two trips. Upstairs, Aunt Helena helped me put the eggs in the ice box. I hurried back down to the woodshed where I had left the jack-in-the-pulpit beside the short-handled shovel Uncle Tee used for clearing the narrow ditch that the kitchen sinks drained into.

The verandah, with its dense covering of hop-vines, was on the east side of the house. At the corner, I went through a narrow gate and then between a stand of tall trees to my right—lilacs and locusts—and some bamboo that reached out from below the verandah railing on my left. I knew what all the plants were because Uncle Tee had told me their names. As I walked out onto the lawn, I could hear Puggy's mop making scrubbing noises but I couldn't see her because the only opening through the hop-vines was at the top of the steps and she was further back.

Uncle Tee had planted two trees halfway out on the lawn, both on the right side. One was a Transparent apple tree, the other a weeping birch. The trunk of the birch had blackened holes all the way from the ground up to the lower limbs, where woodpeckers had drilled into it to get at the insects under the bark. Uncle Tee was afraid the tree was going to die because of this affliction, but it looked pretty tough to me. The whole lawn was level and square, with a fence along each side and a solid cedar hedge at the far end. In the very left corner was a crabapple tree with spreading branches and, in the middle of the hedge, was a very tall elm. The trunk of the elm was so big that no one, not even Uncle Tee or Grandad, could get their arms around it.

127

I angled past the birch tree to the end of the hedge on the right side. The ground sloped down toward the fence and then on down past it to the ditch, with its trickle of water, which ran beside the driveway. Because of the slope, the cedars hadn't been planted right to the end, so I was able to slip between the end of the hedge and the fence. That was the only opening to the area behind the hedge, which was a long, narrow rectangle, the hedge on the one side and a wire fence running along the other three.

I liked the way the word "rectangle" suited it, at least partially: I couldn't think of it as a "wreck" but it was certainly a "tangle." There was a tall cedar back there, on the low side next to the lane, and beside it was a wet, marshy place with cattails and cowslips. There was long grass everywhere and quite a few weeds, mostly burdock and thistle. The most level part was up at the end under the crabapple, where there was actually less grass and fewer weeds because of all the shade. I set the jack-in-the-pulpit down next to the fence and dug the blade of the shovel into the soft ground. This was where my secret garden would be.

From that day on, I spent as much time as I could, between school and chores, and meals and sleep, working on my garden. I still brought some plants home from the places along the shortcut but, mostly, I made trips to our own maple bush, a ten-acre woodlot to the north of the house. Every type of wildflower flourished there, under a high cover of maples, beech, basswood, and even a few pines and spruce. Soon I had the whole upper square under the crabapple blooming with violets, adder tongues, mayflowers, spring beauties, and all the rest. I planted a few trillium as well because I didn't think that transplanting the provincial flower was the same as picking it.

Of course, the garden wasn't really secret, at least not for long. Puggy knew about it right away; before she had even finished the verandah floor, she slipped around the end of the hedge because she was curious about what I was doing. She said, "Oh, I wish I could have a garden too!" When I told her she could share mine, she just shook her head saying, "I don't think Grandma will let me," and turned away. "I'd better get back to my job." Aunt Helena knew too because she was curious as well. She wondered where I disappeared to all the time, so I had to tell her. And she must have told Uncle Tee because one day he gave me one of his old six-quart baskets saying, "Here you go, Brownie. This is pretty wrecked for anything major, but you should be able to use it for transporting your plant stock from the bush."

Sunday morning I came back from a trip to the maple bush with a basketful of moss. I thought I would plant it around all the wildflowers so they would look more natural. I had taken up a few of the violets and mayflowers and one trillium because there wasn't quite enough space for all the moss. Puggy came around the end of the hedge and up through the weeds to where I was.

"It looks so beautiful," she said. "I sure wish I could have a garden of my own." She squatted down beside me.

"Well, why don't you just make one?" I said. "You can have these extra plants that I've taken out. I was going to plant them further over but I don't need to. You could clear a spot anywhere in here and start your own garden right now. There's the shovel and you can get more water down by the cattails in this." I held out the small tin that I had just emptied out on the moss.

"No, I wasn't thinking of in here with yours. But if I could have the plants...." She jumped up and stood facing

129

me. Her eyes were shining. "I know a good place. Come on, I'll show you."

Together we packed the plants into the basket, trying to leave as much earth as possible around the roots. She picked them up and carried them close to her chest, both arms around the basket. I came behind with the shovel, and scooped up a tin of water as we went by the marshy spot.

The place she had chosen was back by the house, in the open spot under the lilacs and locusts. We took turns digging, and when the earth was loose enough, Puggy showed me where she wanted the first plant. I made a deep hole with the blade of the shovel and she poured in some water and then set one of the violets in place. We pressed the soil firmly around it. We did the same with the other two violets and with the mayflowers, one by one. She was standing, the trillium in her hands, looking at the ground. "I think we should put it at the back," she said, "because it's the tallest. I should have thought of that before."

Just as I reached back with the shovel to make the hole, the front door slammed and we heard a thumping noise coming across the verandah floor. We both turned to see Grandma starting down the steps. "Sylvia! You get back in here!" Her huge bulk filled the faded cotton dress, and when she turned and bent down to pick up something, it looked as though the back seams would burst. She came toward us across the lawn. "What do you mean, throwing this down on the floor? Look at the dirt on it!" She held the black book out in front of her. "You're not supposed to be out here anyway. You're supposed to be in reading your Bible on the Sabbath."

Puggy took the Bible with one hand, still holding the trillium tight against her chest with the other. "I didn't throw it...I did my verses...and Grandad said...."

"Never you mind what Grandad said. He's not the one to say."

I laid the shovel down, but immediately I was sorry I did because Grandma shifted her eyes from Puggy to the ground and saw the raw earth and the newly planted wild flowers. "So! this is what you're doing! You come out here on a Sunday and take pleasure for yourself instead of praying and giving praise to our Maker the way I told you to." She took a few steps toward the garden. Again she bent down, the material of her dress stretched in bulges across her buttocks, the bun of grey hair on the top of her head jiggling back and forth. She tore the flowers up out of the earth, first a mayflower, then a violet. She flung them, one by one, out through the lilac trees and over the fence where they landed with a plop in the weedy water of the ditch. "The work of the devil, that's what it is. He finds work for idle hands!" She straightened up finally, her breath coming in gasps out of her toothless mouth. She turned and looked straight at me. "And as for you, you big lump! You may be growing up like a heathen, but your sister won't. I'll see to it that she's raised properly." She whirled and wrenched the trillium from Puggy's grasp. I heard the dull splash as it landed with the others. "Now get back in the house and pray."

That night Aunt Helena finished reading *Black Beauty* to us. The voice of the horse in the very last part stayed in my mind a long time: "and here my story ends. My troubles are all over and I am at home; and often before I am quite

131

awake I fancy I am still in the orchard at Birtwick, standing with my old friends under the apple-trees."

After Aunt Helena had kissed us good night and closed the door, Puggy pulled the covers up tight under her chin. "Bubba, is it all right if I sleep here with you tonight?"

FOURTEEN

POSSESSION WAS SOMETHING I DIDN'T REALLY THINK ABOUT, EVEN though I had acquired quite a few things of my own since coming to live at Rosewood. The first thing really mine was my kitten Topsy. Grown into a sleek length of glossy black fur, she arched herself whenever she saw me, and nearly every night she crawled in under the covers, purring and pushing her head into my hand. But I didn't feel I owned her. I had clothes, of course, and my toothbrush and school books, but the first thing I got that definitely seemed like my own, real possession was a birthday ring. I don't remember ever getting a birthday present before, except for a miniature short-sleeved suit in blue material that my mother made for me when I turned seven. It had its own miniature wooden hanger, and pockets for holding spools of thread and two padded patches at the front for sticking needles and pins into. I liked it a lot but there wasn't much I could do with it since I didn't know how to sew and I didn't own any needles or thread. I probably would have used it when I got older, but it was one of the things that got burned because of the polio.

The morning of my eleventh birthday I sat down to breakfast not suspecting there would be anything special to mark the day. I was just a year older. But there beside my plate was a little packet wrapped in blue tissue paper and tied with a pink ribbon. I pushed it forward a bit as I picked up my fork, not sure it was for me.

Uncle Tee raised his coffee cup and winked. "Happy Birthday, Bubba," he said. "That's for you. Go ahead and open it." He leaned toward Aunt Helena who was still at the stove. "She can open it now, can't she, Helly?"

"Just a minute until I'm sitting down too. You don't want breakfast without potatoes, do you?"

It was a little black box with a lid that was hard to open. Uncle Tee pried it up for me with the tip of his knife. Inside was the most beautiful ring I could ever have imagined. The stone was a chunky rectangle of blue-green, set in a thin gold-coloured frame. Aunt Helena showed me how the ring was split and overlapped so that I could make it the right size. "It's adjustable," she said, and she helped me squeeze it to fit on my middle finger. Then she said, "It's turquoise. That's what the stone is called, and that's the colour too. It's your birthstone." My birthstone. I had never known there was such a thing, never mind that I had one of my own. She explained that it wasn't just mine, that it was the stone for everyone born in December. Hers was diamond because she was born in April; Uncle Tee's was opal for October.

"Then Grandad's is opal too, isn't it?" I knew his

birthday was just two weeks after Uncle Tee's.

"Yes, and your Grandma's is September, so hers is sapphire." Aunt Helena took up a piece of bacon in her fingers and bit off the end.

"Poppy's is sapphire too then, "I said. "What about Puggy's? In June?"

"Oh, that's a nice one. Hers is pearl."

Uncle Tee pushed the last of his potatoes onto the egg already on his fork. "That should be enough talk about birthstones, you two. It doesn't hold water in real life, you know."

I kept looking at the blue-green sparkle of my ring, and twisting it on my finger. Whenever I get any money, I thought, I'm going to get Puggy a pearl ring so she can have a birthstone too.

The idea of possessing things seemed to grow after that. Puggy and I put a claim on all the animals at the barn. Tony was definitely mine, Bert was hers. Since Bette was left over we agreed to share her. We divvied up all the cattle: Becky the Ayrshire was mine; Penny the Jersey was hers; Mollie the blue roan mine; Polly, the Shorthorn hers, and so on through the herd, right down to the last-born of the calves. The sheep, too. We knew all the ewes by name and luckily there were exactly twenty-two, so we halved them as well. Neither one of us wanted the ram, black-faced Michael, because he was so mean, but we shared him anyway. I had the old dog, Snuff, and she had the young one, Nipper; I had Topsy already, she took the mother cat, Sally; and we shared the rest. For the whole year, we kept dividing everything around us into hers and mine. Even when Aunt Ellen and Uncle Ben came up from Toronto on

135

weekends, I claimed Allie as mine and Puggy took the new baby, Benjy. It was a secret; we didn't tell anyone a thing about what we owned.

When Aunt Helena's baby was born it would be mine, because I was the one who lived upstairs; Puggy would have to wait until there was another one. In the last few months Aunt Helena stayed in bed a lot because of the trouble she had the first time, and Uncle Tee got me to do some of the cooking and housework to help out. One morning in mid-February when I got up, the kitchen was empty. There was a note on the table. "Gone to hospital. Milking done, and feeding, except for sheep and hens. Stoke up the fire before you leave for school. We'll probably have our baby by the time you get home." It was signed "U.T."

It was a long day at school for Puggy and me; the walk home that time of year was the long way around by road and of course it had snowed all day just to make the road worse. As we climbed through the drifts at the top of the rise by Old Ed's maple bush, we could see Uncle Tee coming down the lane with the team on the snow plough. The snow wasn't so deep from there on so we ran the rest of the way.

"Yessir," Uncle Tee said. "Everything's fine. Your Aunt Helena's got her baby girl."

It was difficult to take in the fact that there was going to be a baby in the house. The Soldiers' Memorial Hospital did not allow children to visit so we had to content ourselves with news of her through Uncle Tee. He went to town every morning and again every evening. We knew that her name was Leslie (they hadn't decided on a middle name yet), she was seven pounds two ounces at birth, she had dark hair, and she was healthy. I hadn't said anything to Puggy yet about claiming her.

Aunt Helena wasn't to come home for a week at least, but before even two days passed, Grandma landed in the hospital too. She had gone to town with Uncle Tee in the morning because it was Friday and that was the day she delivered to customers—town people who preferred her country eggs and home-made butter to what they could get in the stores. Grandad was sick with a bad bout of asthma so Grandma made Puggy stay home from school to look after him. She said she couldn't disappoint her customers. The eggs were fine but it was a surprise to me that anyone could like her butter, never mind prefer it and even pay to have it. She used too much salt after churning and over-dosed the batch with "Marigold" colouring, so if a plate of it sat for a while and got too warm, yucky crystals would form on the surface and stand out like white grainy growths on the almost orange background. It made me think of pictures I had seen of the Fly Amanita in a book Uncle Tee had on mushrooms. It was "brilliant scarlet or orange, ... and usually covered by whitish or creamy warts." The reason for its name was that this mushroom was used "for killing houseflies." Grandma's butter would sure kill houseflies, I thought. Aunt Jane always brought their own from Barrie, and at the table, even if he was sitting right next to Grandma, Mint would say, "Pass the creamery butter, please." Because of Grandma's butter, I had stopped eating butter of any kind—back when we first came from the West—and several of our cousins had cut it out altogether too, for the same reason.

Now Grandma was in the hospital because of a terrible

137

nosebleed she had in the women's washroom of the library by the old Opera House theatre. Someone took her there, someone who knew that Aunt Helena had just had her baby and that Uncle Tee was visiting her. "High blood pressure," Uncle Tee said when he got home and told us. "She's going to have to stay in for a while."

It was Sunday when we got the news. Uncle Tee had gone to town to see them both at the hospital. I went downstairs to help Puggy and to keep her and Grandad company. Puggy was stoking the fire in the dining room where Grandad sat bundled up in his rocker. She was doing her best to keep Grandad occupied because he was so worried about Grandma. She had already read him the newest episode of a story they had been following in *The Winnipeg Free Press*, something that Grandma did not allow at all, even on weekdays. They always had to take whatever chance they could to read it. He sat by the stove, head bowed, opening and closing his hands in his lap. Puggy sat beside him, asking him questions about the old days, trying to get him to talk to take his mind off the worry. When she asked how he and Grandma first met, he raised his head and his eyes brightened.

138

"I was driving along the road on a load of hay. And there she was walking alone, the prettiest skip of a girl you can imagine. She had a bouquet of flowers—well, they weren't any decent flowers at all, just a bunch of goldenrod. I stopped the team and asked her if she'd like a ride. She clambered up onto the hay like nothing I'd ever seen, still with that bunch of yellow in one hand. I took her along to where she was staying. She was related to the people a few farms away. I didn't have the heart to tell her she'd been picking weeds."

"How did you get to see her again? Did you go to church or anything?"

"Oh, mostly I just gave her rides on the wagon." He smiled. Then he pulled the shawl closer with both hands and added, "She didn't turn religious until later on, after we got married." He bowed his head again. Puggy gave me a desperate look, turning her palms upward to let me know she had run out of ideas.

To help her out, I said I'd give the hospital a call and find out how Grandma was doing. It would cheer Grandad up to know she was getting better. I went to the kitchen, rang Central and gave her the number. When I told the voice at the other end that I wanted to enquire about my grandmother, Mrs. Cassidy in Room 402, there was a long silence. Then the voice came on again: "I am sorry to tell you, but Mrs. Cassidy passed away about half an hour ago."

I motioned to Puggy from the door. Grandad did not raise his head, apparently unaware that I had been on the phone. When I told her, she said, "We can't let him know. We'd better wait for Uncle Tee; he can tell him." Then she went to the pantry and brought out bread and butter and two eggs. She spooned bacon grease into a pan and cracked the eggs. "I'll get him to eat something. He sure won't want to eat once he's heard the news."

As we stood at the stove, her scrambling the eggs and me turning the bread to make toast, we whispered, "Grandma's dead. She's really dead." We started laughing, and we held onto each other and it was a long time before we could stop. But Grandad didn't hear us. Puggy moved the pan to the back of the stove. She arranged the egg and

139

toast on a plate and took it in to him and we helped him move to a chair by the table. I watched her as she stood with one hand on his shoulder, offering him the first forkful, and all I could think was how we had never tried to possess any of the adults in our lives. Even though he was now our only grandparent in the world, it wouldn't be right to mention claiming him. The new baby would be mine, but Grandad definitely belonged to Puggy.

FIFTEEN

I WAS LEARNING A LOT ABOUT STORIES AND ESSAYS AT SCHOOL, and during one special hour once a week the teacher read some chapters from a book. First it was *Swiss Family Robinson* and then *Masterman Ready*. It was for the whole school, from grade one up to grade eight, and all twenty-nine of us could hardly wait for three o'clock Friday afternoons. I liked poetry best, though. Since I was the only one in Grade Eight, the teacher let me choose most of the poems and we read them and talked about them. My favourite one was "The Highwayman." I liked the galloping rhythm of "The highwayman came riding, riding, riding...." I had tried to write poetry myself, so I knew how hard it was. When I didn't know what to write about Aunt Helena said I should think of something familiar, something right around home. My first poem was about a tomato:

A tomato is rosy red,
It has no body, only a head.
It grows from a vine, it lives on the ground.
It never is square, but usually round.

The next one was about a cat who "sleeps upon the sheepskin mat," and after that I wrote horse poems and cow poems and poems about flowers and pussy willows and one about seagulls who "with their cries come following the plough."

When I made up poems, I wrote them on whatever sheets of wrapping paper were around because I had to keep making changes. Once they were finished I wrote them out neatly and put them in a loose-leaf binder. I stripped some bark from the biggest birch tree in the maple bush to make a cover. The white bark made the binder more special and romantic. Over time the poems got longer and were about more complicated things. My last poem told the story of an evil spell, a tragic love, and two birch trees with "their branches intertwined." It had ten verses, one of which was this sad conclusion:

A birch tree was the gallant knight
And now the lady stood
Her arms stretched to her husband
As she was changed to wood

142

I began to worry that I was running out of things to write about; I hadn't really had much to do yet with tragic love, evil spells, and intertwined arms.

But I thought ahead to when Aunt Helena would have

her baby, and bring it home. I would have a whole new subject. I could write a long series of baby poems, maybe one for every day, or at least one a week.

Because Grandma died while Aunt Helena was still in hospital with the baby, everything at home changed. After the funeral the aunts and uncles gathered in the dining-room at Rosewood to talk about what to do. Grandad was not well enough to be on his own, even with Puggy's help, and Aunt Helena wouldn't be able to take on two extra people, either upstairs or downstairs; she wasn't well yet and she had her first baby to care for. Grandad went to live with Aunt Jane in Barrie. Uncle Tee and Aunt Helena had been making installments on the farm; now the whole house was theirs.

Uncle Tee wanted to have most of the move downstairs over by the time Aunt Helena came home with the baby. He and the aunts and uncles decided what things of Grandma's to divide among themselves, such as the furniture, the bedding, and the pictures, and what to give to the grandchildren. Aunt Jane had already packed all the things Grandad would need, and since Grandma's clothes were too big for anyone else, she took them all to Barrie to give to the Mission. Puggy and I got her Singer sewing machine between us but neither one of us knew how to use it. We also shared the books in the little wall cupboard in the dining-room, old books that were our father's. We had read them already—*Robin Hood, Struggling Upward, Try Again, Curing Christopher*—but we liked having books of our own and especially books that had been his. There was a small ceramic horse that had been his too. Poppy had always wanted to play with it whenever she was at

143

Rosewood, so Aunt Mae took it home for her.

The biggest job was re-arranging the kitchen. Aunt Helena told Uncle Tee how she wanted things to be. She certainly didn't want the crock of smelly sauerkraut that always stood on the floor in the pantry, or the empty honey pails and gunny sacks that cluttered up the cupboards, or the stinky commode that was in what was going to be the baby's room. She wanted all her own red-trimmed kitchen furniture to be moved downstairs; she would worry about repainting the walls and wainscoting and built-in parts later, maybe in the spring. She sent notes home to me about packing the dishes, cutlery, pots and pans in boxes for the move, and then putting them all back in their proper places; the same for the contents of the icebox. Puggy helped me with everything. As we made trip after trip the change became more and more real to us.

"It's really going to be different, isn't it?" I said, as I put the last of the tea towels and potholders in place. "I don't mean just moving down here, but having Leslie home." I was trying to get used to calling her Leslie.

"Well, I'm going to miss Grandad, but it'll sure be great to have the baby," Puggy said. She turned from scrubbing the sink. "I can't wait to see her and to have Poppy see her." She sloshed the dishcloth up and down. "But the best part is that we get to be together again. All the time, I mean."

Aunt Helena had all Leslie's clothes ready. Some of them were sweaters and bootees and bonnets she had knit for Barbara Carol, the baby that had miscarried. She also had blankets and towels, powder and diapers, and everything else, even a little white bathtub. There was also a crib and buggy that had been Allie's and then Benjy's that Aunt Ellen had sent up, and a high chair Uncle Tee had made.

When the day arrived, Puggy and I didn't have to go to school. Uncle Tee said we should be there to give Aunt Helena some help when she got home. "I'll bet you two are pretty anxious to meet our little girl," he said, his eyes twinkling like Grandad's. "She'll be a little sister for you. She's quite a beauty." After he left, we swept and dusted and made everything tidy, then we changed our clothes. I gave Puggy some of my clothes—slacks and a pullover. When she put on the slacks, she jumped up and down and shouted, "Look at me, Grandma! Look at me! I'm wearing pants!"

"Aunt Helena will even let you wear shorts," I said. "In the summer, I mean. And no more long stockings!"

I made a pot of coffee and set it on the stove to perk. Puggy put out four cups and saucers and the sugar bowl and cream pitcher. Then we pulled chairs up to the window and watched for the red truck to appear over the rise down by the maple bush on Old Ed's place.

I was ready to start writing poems as soon as I got to see the baby but, as happened so many times before, things turned out to be very different from what I expected.

When I saw Leslie on the kitchen table, lying on a big pillow Aunt Helena had warmed for her at the stove, I didn't feel I needed to write poetry any more. She had dark hair, violet blue eyes, long lashes, a rose-petal mouth, full round cheeks, translucent skin, dancing hands, and long, perfect limbs; she was a poem, all by herself. "We want her second name to be Kathleen, after your mother," Aunt Helena said. "I never met your mother but everyone liked her so much, except your Grandma, of course, and it would be nice for our child to be her namesake."

"Kathleen was a special person, with a 'heart of gold,' as they say," Uncle Tee said. "Since none of you got her name, we thought our little girl should have the honour. Is it okay with you?"

I remembered how, when we all lived at Uncle Court's place, our father would sing: "I'll take you home again Kathleen." He sang: "Across the country far and wide / To where your heart has ever been / Since first you were my bonny bride." Puggy was nodding vigorously. I did the same.

"That's it then, Helly," Uncle Tee said. He carefully raised the baby out of my lap and held her up so that her cheek touched his. "So, it's Leslie Kathleen. How do you like your name, little one?" She gurgled and we all laughed. "Leslie Kathleen it is then."

Not only did I no longer need to write poetry about her, I had no time, for she filled our days. When we weren't at school or doing chores or sleeping, we were with her, helping Aunt Helena with feeding, bathing, powdering, changing diapers, holding, rocking, and even just watching her sleep.

146

Everyone said she looked like her father, which made Uncle Tee's eyes sparkle. He liked to sit at the table while she was being changed, or just being fussed over by the rest of us, and let her fingers curl like tendrils around his thumb. "Look how strong she is already!" he would say and lift his hand to show how she hung on. "Strong enough to milk cows!"

When I had her to myself I read her poems and stories. By the time she was a month old, Puggy and I carried her to the barn through the snow to show her the animals—Tony, Bert, and Bette, the cows, the calves, the sheep and pigs, even the chickens. And we sang out the ways to call them all, so she would know how when she was old enough. "Co-boss! Co-boss!" and "Sookie, Sookie, Sookie!" and "Pig, Pig, Pig!" and "Nanny, Nanny, Nanny!" and "Chickie, Chickie, Chickie!" and, somewhere in between, the way to whistle for the horses. During the rest of March and into April we pushed her in the buggy up and down the lane and told her about the wildflowers that would come up soon. I pointed toward my secret garden behind the hedge and Puggy stopped dead still. She said, "Hey! Now I can have *my* garden!"

Easter was very late that year; Good Friday was the twelfth of April. Thursday was our last day of school before the holidays. Aunt Helena had had a cold for several days and wasn't feeling well, so she asked Puggy and me to take the baby while she got a little rest before supper. I poured orange juice for Puggy to take to Aunt Helena and then heated a bottle of milk for Leslie Kathleen. We both sat with her by the stove. Puggy held her first; when it was my turn, I raised her to my shoulder for a burp. Her head was right beside my ear and I could hear her making little snuffling noises. I said to Puggy, "I think she's getting a cold too."

The next morning, Good Friday, Aunt Helena was feeling worse and stayed in bed; when Puggy and I came in from chores she said Leslie seemed to be sick too. "She's

147

quite pale and kind of listless."

Uncle Tee came in and sat on the bed beside Aunt Helena. "Leslie seems to have trouble breathing," he said. He put his fingertips to her forehead, then felt her pulse. "Maybe it's something more than a cold."

Uncle Tee had almost finished medical school and so, I thought, if something was serious he would know, and I'm sure Aunt Helena had the same thought because she said, "If you think so, then we'd better do something right now."

"I'll get her to the doctor. Puggy, hand us those blankets." While Aunt Helena wrapped Leslie in several layers, Uncle Tee turned to Puggy: "You stay here and keep your aunt company." To me he said, "You, Tom, get your coat and boots. You'll have to come with me to hold Leslie."

In the truck, I wrapped my arms tight around her. Why did Uncle Tee keep giving me new nicknames? First he called me "Brownie," because of my dress. Next was "Twink" because of how my eyes crinkled up when I laughed, he said. The winter before, I got hit by a snowball, and he called me "Shiner" for a while, even after the black around my eye went away. Lately he called me "Thomas Aquinas," which he often shortened to "Tom." When I asked him why "Thomas Aquinas," he just smiled and said, "Aquinas was a philosopher, a seeker after truth—like you." To find out more, I looked him up in the encyclopedia. I didn't understand his ideas, but part of the entry stayed with me a long time: "St. Thomas Aquinas was known as the 'Angelic Doctor,' and by his school companions as 'the Dumb Ox,' because he was slow in manner and quite

stout." I wasn't slow and I wasn't very stout but there in
the cab beside Uncle Tee, with Leslie snuffling in my ear, I
earnestly wished I could be an "angelic doctor" for her.

                        ⬬

    When we got back to Rosewood, Aunt Helena jumped
out of bed when she saw we didn't have the baby. Uncle
Tee put his arms around her but she pushed them away.
"Where's Leslie? What's wrong with her?"

    "Doctor Cunningham knew it was serious when
he examined her. He put her in an ambulance and she's
already on her way to the Sick Children's Hospital. We'll
drive down to the city right away."

    Aunt Helena sat down hard on the bed. "What's
wrong?"

    "He's pretty sure it's leukemia."

    "How can she be sick? She's never been sick. Everyone
who sees her says she's 'the picture of health.'"

    And Uncle Tee said, "It isn't definite yet. Let's just go.
The sooner we get there the better."

    I helped Aunt Helena pack a suitcase. Uncle Tee gave
Puggy and me instructions about everything that needed
doing. He got Murray on the phone and I felt better
knowing he would help us with the main chores morning
and evening. As I came out of the bedroom I heard Uncle
Tee say, "I'm afraid so, Murr. It looks like sunset for our
little girl." Aunt Helena didn't hear him; she was in the
bedroom, pulling her navy blue dress over her head.

    Grandma had made us pray whenever she could, and
while Uncle Tee and Aunt Helena were gone, I prayed lots
of times, wherever I was—in the house or the barn or the

149

henhouse. I prayed to God and to Jesus to let Leslie live: please don't let there be a "sunset" for her. Don't take her away from Aunt Helena and Uncle Tee. If you have to take someone, take me. I can go instead because my mother is already there, and Leslie means so much to my aunt and uncle.

Easter Sunday. Every year on Easter Sunday Grandma would stand at the bottom of the front stairs and call up to Uncle Tee. "Walter!" she would shout. (She was the only one who called him by his real name.) "Walter!" She would wait for him to answer and then would call, "Have you heard the good news?" And he would always say, "No. What's that?" (We couldn't believe he fell for it every year.) "Christ has risen!"

Not this Easter Sunday. We heard the three long rings that were our number, and rushed to the phone. I took down the receiver and held it so that Puggy could hear too. Uncle Tee's voice was low and far away. He said, "I'm sorry, girls; Leslie didn't make it."

I hung up the receiver and leaned against the wall. Leslie was dead and I was still alive. Through tears, I looked out the window at a grey, empty sky. Puggy hugged me and cried, too, then she said, "Let's put away Leslie's stuff. They'll be here in a couple of hours. It'll be too hard on Aunt Helena to see all her things."

150

We took down the diapers and shirts that had been hung to dry on a line over the stove. We gathered up the woolly sweaters and bonnets and bootees and folded them into the carriage along with the pastel blankets and lacy pillow. We piled the soaps and powders and creams on top of the towels in the bathtub and pushed it down on top of the buggy and wheeled it into the pantry and closed the door. We couldn't put the crib out of sight, so Puggy covered it with one of Grandma's big patchwork quilts. Then we built up the fire and put coffee on the stove to perk.

❧

Aunt Helena's sister drove home with them. She said, "Look how neat the girls have got everything!"

"It's too darn neat!" Aunt Helena said; she burst into tears and ran into the bedroom.

Uncle Tee helped Auntie Nora out of her coat and took off his own. "It's an empty, empty house," he said.

And the house was still empty when Leslie came back into it. She was in the far corner of the dining room, in a small, white, sculpted casket. I approached her slowly. She still looked perfect. I bent to kiss her cheek and was shocked by its hardness. I remembered the time Aunt Millie kissed me for the first time and where I had expected stone I felt her soft, wrinkled skin pushing into my cheek. Now, the opposite.

How had Puggy found mayflowers? It was far too early. How did she get them into Leslie's hand?

No words. Leslie Kathleen my poem—my dead poem.

The funeral was to be private. Aunt Helena said she didn't want people to come. They'd probably attend out of curiosity, and she couldn't tolerate that. Uncle Tee simply turned all the chairs in the room to face the wall.

❧

Behind the hedge, the long narrow necks of the cattails, now brown and dry, were held upright by collars of ice. "Grandma was wrong," I thought. "There is no God, or

Lord, or Jesus!" How surprised Grandma must have been when she found nothing there, no heaven, nothing. But if so, where was our mother? Our heart-of-gold mother. Kathleen.

My eyes burned, cold and anguished.

≈

In my secret garden, clumps of mayflower pushed up through snow. Some just in bud, some in bloom.

> Spring's icy dreams will never melt,
>   though sleeping life begins to stir:
> The mayflowers that she would have picked,
>   instead were picked for her.

PEGEEN BRENNAN WAS BORN IN ASHCROFT, IN BRITISH COLUMBIA'S Cariboo region, but spent most of her childhood years in Ontario.

She taught English Literature at the University of British Columbia for twenty-two years. Since taking early retirement, she and her husband live in Kilpoola, B.C., near Osoyoos.

Her fiction and poetry have appeared in various literary magazines; she has published two novels, *Zarkeen* and *Big Rock Candy Town*, and three books of poetry.

Cover photos: The house is Rosewood Farm in North Orillia Township, former home of the Brennan family.

The two insets are of the author at ages six and twelve.

ISBN 1-41204752-8

9 781412 047524